Witch-Blood

Volume 1

By Wix Solis

Contents

Chapter 1. A Witch's Desperation

‘No No No, back at the orphanage, it's not possible'. Thoughts of how fucked she was drowned her mind. Why did she feel this way; limited, less, foggy, fucked. Where was Querf?! Everyone warned her against choosing such a dark creature as a familiar. Whilst she would remind him of that a great deal, she never revealed to him he had never truly failed her, not when it mattered. Never, until now. Now, thoughts of regret broke her pride. Shock stumbled her as she realised, she didn't miss his skills but him, the little twat he was.

The space she was in was large, alas a single room, no separating walls. Rusty beds without mattresses, one window and not much else. She floundered over to her old bed, The one closest to the window. She rubbed the frame, specifically, over the scratches her past self-had made, a tally. It made her notice herself.

She looked down at her hands, naked of ring and trinket, all relics and help absent from her wrists. With the panic bore film of sweat upon her dark skin thickening she made the book summoning symbols. With both hands forming fists but one hand forming a fist with index finger outstretched and the other fist three fingers outstretched; her lock. As she brought hands together and muttered the secret word she had anchored as the magical key, nothing happened. She tried again, However, the book didn't open itself into existence, bewildered, her eyes remained where it should be levitating but wasn't. Her panic gave birth to desperation which she felt as deep as her bones.

" Okay, what the 'eck is going on, I thought no f..." Her out-loud self-defiance was interrupted by a boom beyond thunder. The unearthly sound was bore from an unknown force hitting the whole left side of the building. So hungry a force, the window and its frame shattered, spitting out its vitreous teeth onto the stone floor.

Thoughts that the building was collapsing consumed her, but it didn't. As she opened her eyes, she saw the door had splintered but still held. Though only unbroken due to the sigil it wore. However, now the blood which made the paint had a much deeper rue. Sophia could see it was one of her own design, one of the first blood-sigils she ever learned, a simple but powerful non-entry spell. Its glow now dim it remained active but was fading. Her head spun with pain as she tried with all her might to remember making it. She couldn't. She could barely picture the moment before and had no more time as the imminent future demanded her minds presence.

She threw off her concerns, the tiny truth she held onto was that her little shield was keeping the awful dark out there and this pleased her, it gave her just enough time to make a choice.

But what was she even fighting? She thought she knew but now could not remember. 'Why was she even fighting? and why alone!?' none of it mattered. She wiped the fear from her face and got ready for war. Her mind spoke to her; 'Time to be smart not scared.' With this new ice in her veins, she coaxed herself to fall on to her knees. Her plan was desperate, but desperation was something known all too well. She knew it was on the verge of impossible, almost lunacy, but she hated the helplessness imposed on her and it seemed better than the guaranteed prey she was.

Orphan-mother Privy's voice sung in Sophia's head, one of her slogans spoken so many times she saw it as a part of her rather than a mantra;

"If you listen, the world will whisper to you what you can and cannot do…"

It gave her idea an idea. Her plan would fail if her body was frozen or too desperate, so she couldn't rush it. The panic would use more of her energy and the final remnants come the end will be needed. It had to be done another way, mind-state always influenced action. She was trying to stop the sea for a moment, about to ask the sky to open just for her. It had to be done right.

Her breathing had quietened and whilst not smiling her face was no longer tight, whilst not relaxed she cared less than she did. She almost jumped to her feet. Walking over to one of the shards of glass on the floor, she scooped it up with gumption. She thought to herself a final time about how crazy she was.

'It's going to take almost every drop I have, and I've only seen it once, no room for error, but then again what'dya expect.'

She cut her wrist deeply with the cabins tooth. Though so used to incision, with her whole body covered in scars, this felt different. She drew a little blood for a little help, she was a blood witch but this was mutilation. This did not stop her but was seen as the extra cost for what she wanted. As she drew the large circle from the stream that fell from her, she felt her energy leave her as if a river, but she could not stop. Instead, she closed her eyes and pictured the orphanage garden. She saw the trees all moving in unison: breathing and dancing lives in their own respect. As she went on to breath in and out, she saw within herself; she saw her lungs as these trees, the leaves her alveoli, the whole garden, the whole world inside her chest helping her breathe and keeping her calm. This introspective echo she held onto tightly as she felt her hands speed up with the patterns they were drawing within the circle. Solomon squares, Alchemy crossovers and even the ancient projected forms, everything she found difficult done as if simple. All of Sofia's resistance eroded away but so was every other part of her and if she failed any remnants of this resistance left behind were worthless to her. Again, it did not matter now, her attempt was nearly done. Then she would either have the power she needed or at least be allowed to give in to the creeping weight of slumber saturating her.

The roof was torn from the building, wind raged around the room with the sky its partner; alight with lighting, living flames of green, red and blue crossing over to form putrid purples and blinding yellows. She felt the gaze of something beyond size looking down on her, but it didn't matter, she had no more life in her. She fell using her last life's choice to throw her hand towards the activating circle at the top of her design rather than kneel or break her fall. As her body lay ex-animate the sigil set alight brighter than the sky above, it shone in defiance dwarfing the skies fury. The flame the blood had become burned a wonder-some whitened red, silver flickering in its core. All the scratches, the shapes inside the circle slithered to the outside thickening the sigils perimeter until the flaming circle surrounding Sofia was empty but for her. Then as if atmospheric pressure was abounding the fire-blood took accelerated return to her veins, filling her with magic flame. She breathed in strongly, though she has been wasting her lungs 'till now and rose to her feet, then levitated off the ground. Godhood was in her veins but for how long, she felt it burning her away, but she had more than she needed, more than enough power, she could do anything.

Now she calmed herself for new reason, she was getting drunk on possibility, the problem above her in comparison to before was nothingness, ant sized. Now she had new choices to make. However, before she could act the room began to melt away. Then when surrounded by nothing but blankness she allowed herself to also be enveloped, to melt away too and closing her eyes everything went black.

Chapter 2. The Masters Meeting

Arthur felt small. Disgraced to be the reason his pupil was being whipped up into a self-concocted fear. For no other reason than to have knowledge of her. And over her. All the masters were agreed; to lie to their students and hope their dreams fade away, as common with the dream-time ritual. To be part of that, part of a group thirstily watching an unconscious girl laid upon an ancient, mirrored floor, Blasé about discussing her private dreams as she fights them. Regardless of the encroaching threat it was wrong to him, but he was outvoted, as always. He was from a time before most of theirs, before this one. If it was his choice he would've been left behind, warriors don't want to be old, especially over 200 years.

The other masters back and fourths were murmurous to him as he pondered. So, he let his mind wander further. Maybe it was because his eyes already wore guilt, but he saw her as a girl and not his disciple. Always so fierce and fiery, her intent-full, forceful motions gone. No hair, hat or hand covering her face. Her shoulder length blackish hair currently in pigtail double braids, accentuating her feminine feel. If he looked at her sleeping form and not past her to what she was doing in the mirror; he saw how sweetly round her cheeks were. How button her nose. How suited her eyebrows; arresting and well-formed, not bushy but perfect for non-verbal communication. The girl's shoulders sloped down, so quite whilst wide they were deceivingly so. She was athletically slender; Arthur believed her forms acquisition obvious with her forehead bearing many unrelated to magic marks. He looked further; saw how the scars of her face were few and shallow but the two on the neck deep. One deep chest mark, then many upon her wrists and hands. He wandered what the pattern of scars looked like under the clothes, but it was platonic. More to the end of knowing if in selective clothes she may look unblemished, if she could hide in a quiet life. She was attractive but he was so past carnal relations, even in his first life he swore off women to focus on becoming a great force for good. Come this second life forced upon him, he didn't even remember what those inclinations felt like. The recoils of his former life also wore at him physically. As he clutched the stump of his right elbow; he wondered if the phantom burning of his arm was something poignant to these thoughts or if he had been so deep in himself he hadn't noticed the pain. Regardless, he gently rubbed it in a slow soothing manner, like how a man twiddled his beard when chewing on his thoughts. The change in stance was enough for the other masters to notice his absence in their conversion. With the bearded pirate and behemoth of a man directly opposite Arthur beginning the parade of comments;

"You ain't said nuttin' One-arm, you see what your crazy bitch's trying to do!?" Zarros proclaimed.

"It is a forbidden ritual she shouldn't know about, Arthur" said softly the woman aside Zarros.

As she spoke, her eyes swiftly flicked up off the mirror-floor to try meet Arthur's eyes then back to it, they cared not to have failed. They let him know she was onto his potential miscreance. He did not care; 'Those green eyes and green skin, they match her green as grass naivety.' Whilst he ignored her, with his gaze remaining transfixed on Sophia, Arthur did raise his eyes a few heartbeats later to look up at Yenya, whom he knew was also going to speak. His eyebrows raised involuntarily, alas slightly, they made his face disregarding as he listened to his friend's gravelled voice, the one he used in public;

"She's going to succeed." Yenya whispered, though his voice still cut the room with its depth. His familiar, currently in the form of Lark, returning to his shoulder as if to grow his aura of dominion. The bird's eyes never left Arthur as it landed but Yenya's never left the mirror.

" FUCK OFF, IF SHE CAN DO THAT THERE IT'S CONFIRMED LETS JUS …."
Zarros began Bellowing. Spit spluttering from his lips down his black and grey beard. Though he cut his own proclamation short as he had noticed Yenya had started to move around the sleeping girl and towards him, though his eyes kept down, watching Sophia's dream; the circle of blood around her was now alight, confirming Yenya's suspicions.

"You're making me think your heart still wants to negotiate with the threat" Yenya said as he reached Zarros, putting his hand gently on his shoulder.

Zarros was far bigger than Yenya and his thick muscles tightened at the contact, his teeth gritted with such strength they looked liable to shatter in his mouth; but he had heard the stories told world over and his eyes had seen Yenya complete feats beyond him therein themselves. No man could dominate him, but the council head was more than a man. So, the Pirate-king did what came hardest to him. He surrendered.

" We need to end this" Cassandra demanded. As she spoke, she walked over to and behind Zarros whom huffed in accordance, her closeness jolting his mind back into the room, his shoulder shunting Yenya's hand from his by aggressive jut.

Arthur's eyes greedily gulped in the scene; even the threat of violence had conflict, and this thrilled him. The opposition of the two men had Arthur think on his own aging form. Inspecting Yenya he saw how only Zarros could dwarf him, he was still so tall. Unlike his own tatty attire, his friend wore clothes a hundred years more modern, brown one coloured leather, long with many pockets. Sophia often said he himself had a grandfatherly face whereas Yenya he knew was desired by many women, all his junior. It was plain why, his skin was aged but the wrinkles few and shallow, his hair more silver than white; still pristine and thick. The way it was longer on one side was almost vampiric. This longer side often a flap overhanging to cover a side of his forehead and upper face. Women love the peacocking the old man thought.

Whereas his own face he barely recognised when he saw it gawping back from the mirrored floor. So many wrinkles which even he himself found impossible to distinguish; to tell if they were new furrow or antiqued scar. Arthur touched his bulbous nose and ruminated on its old shape. His friend's nose was large from age too but not wide, longer and more sloped, distinguished. The shoulders not wide but not many would know from how he used his height. His beard was greyer than the molten silver of his hair, more like stone and perkily kept in an inverted triangle that entirely covered his mouth. He did not want anyone to know his speech's what's and when's or witness its micro-expressions. Arthur was confident he could read him regardless. The master of moon and sun's ears were smaller than his own, medium sized and pinned back naturally but entirely; this along with his nose gave an avarian and predatory energy to his presence. Like he was thousands of yards above us all. Scratching his own head in a comforting assessment the difference between him and his friend further burned at him; the elder man still had hair but not a lot so kept it buzzed, his wide ears no longer able to be hidden by said hair. His looks went a long, long, time ago. Now people looked at him like he was never young. His barrel head no longer the sign of a warrior but now a fool. Arthur felt the twinge as he kept both his eyes open. Both worked but two intersecting scars of different battles traced and crossed his left eye. As often, relenting, he began squinting with it. He continued watching, knowing irrespective of it was going to explode or subside, that moment was now.

Yenya ignored the aggressive slight knowing Zarros' inclination for impulsive action could slow down the day. However, he finally looked up from the mirror, his gaze speedily meeting Zarros before being held on Arthur.

" I can smell your curiosity my apathetic friend, I share it, but we don't know enough Arthur... What if it's the final wear and tear needed? You know were not ready and one wrong step now will crush us." Warmth accompanied the inherent dominance in his tone this time.

With all three masters' now on the opposite side of the sleeping girl to him Arthur's reply came without warmth, instead his usual cadence; slowly spoken but well enunciated; indifferent:

"Fine, but know your disciples are no different, think of your own youths. The only thing we've learned from all these dreams is we now know my student is on a higher level than Zarros' creepy twins, Cassy's wimpy siblings or even your cherished Sun and Moon." His accompanying gesture even closer matched the content of his words than his tone as he straightened his only arm and defiantly swept over Sophia's head as if he held ceremonial sword. Coinciding was muttering something known only to him. The mirror gradually faded black then sharply inverted back to reflective form.

Albeit to different levels, all three masters took displeasure with these words; with halted hisses, snarls and more all coming from the unlikely pack. All further words were held for now however as Sophia had begun to come too and appearances around the young were oh so important in their upholding. The four masters studied the girl eagerly to see if she would remember the ordeal; Sophia's face was crunched up with the transitional tension. Her eyes opened. Both the blue one and the red one were filled with deranged glee from the situation before, then confusion, then pain. She closed her eyes tightly to deal with it, then her eyelids

15

softened, her face relaxed and she opened them lightly. This time herself.

The girl shot up to a sitting position whilst equipping her secret bone-knife bracelet, but she realised her surroundings before any incision or incantation were begun. Zarros couldn't help but smile at the girls reflex to fight.

Approaching the girl, wearing his steely smile the Pirate King offered his hand out declaring;

"Fuck the Blood magic! Join me, my child. I have chaos items that would spin your head…" His voice playful.

Sophia was cycling her gaze between his black eyes and offered gold-drenched hand. Her lip was upturned ever so, unnoticed by Zarros, this may as well have been a grimace to Arthur, who knew she didn't enjoy being called child and had not really considered his offer yet. Arthur did not want her considering the offer, he knew his student was a good person, but he equally knew she was quick to anger, with this intoxicating her mind in so many situations. Not having moved, he was already standing by the girl but to her back. He loudly followed Zarros making the girl spin around sharply, to see his only hand also being offered to help her up;

"She is a blood-witch and I don't think she's looking for a King to protect". Arthur's reply was cunning and his tone matching.

The girl looked atop her shoulder back at Zarros who had said no more, hand still out, smile widening. Then past him, Cassandra and Yenya were standing by the door, Cassandra quietly berating the council's head. When Cassandra saw Sophia was looking, she stopped her frantic verbal whispers, opened the door whilst holding eye contact with her then left the room. At the loud shutting of the heavy metal door Zarros' hand dropped and he swung his enormous body around. Seeing Cassandra had left he strode across the mirrored floor towards the door himself, rushed but not panicked his steps making a twanged ping as they hit the floor with force. He shouted back as he moved;

"Open offer!" This was trailed by roaring laughter.

" Asshole." Arthur grumbled.

A chuckle came from the girl as she spun her head back around and grabbed his hand in one swift motion. Now back in her swing, she easily shot herself up to her feet. She was small, so when she pulled herself up Arthur was more than enough of an anchor. Not moving despite being so much less than he used to be.

Yenya had walked over to Arthur, bumping into him playfully as he reached him. Though now all standing Yenya had to look down at his elderly friend and the tired witch. With a well-practised smile, he made attempt to comfort the girl;

"Well done today, you surprised us if not your master. Now run along and get some sleep...or gossip if you prefer, but real explanations come tomorrow". A wink accompanied the suggestion.

Arthur winced inside like the eye shot an arrow; the words were not just for her but his friend's subtle way of telling him he's disappointed for the missing honesty between them. Alas, Yenya was too logical, and Arthur didn't want him calculating just yet. The one-armed warlock usually enjoyed when the celestial master' had subtle coherences hidden just for him in words spoken for others, but not today. Arthur made great effort to hold face and not drop his head.

" Thank you Yenya, I, err.." Sophia's awkward words were complemented by a toothless smile. She like everyone had a great reverence for Yenya, seeing him as more legend than man. Not many people could shake Sophia's conviction and Arthur wondered if she would hold him as highly in her mind's eye if she knew as much about Yenya as he did. It's not that he didn't respect his friend but was more than aware of his mortal imperfections.

Sophia's quizzed expression showed she was still thinking about how best to respond but Yenya took the pause as a chance to halt the stumbling and announce his departure;

"I have business to attend to before my bird flips, as I like to say. Regardless, I'm sure you both have thoughts to barter. Always best done in private". His words came with a chortle.

With this he gracefully moved towards the door, as quickly as Zarros but without the accompanying cacophony. As he left, he sent Arthur a telepathic message. This was rare for several reasons;

"I'm no Bentham but you can't deny the similarity between the situations. Remember your obligatory master." The foreign thought echoed unpleasantly in Arthur's mind quieter each time until it dispersed.

Before he reached the door, he began maundered incarnations to himself. They were too quiet to discern properly. Yet in the strange silence ambient to this room, they were loud enough for Sophia to hear they sounded like Egyptian Sun magic. Ending as he reached the exit which opened itself but not to reveal the long many-doored corridor to the water-hall but instead a portal. Creating a portal was very difficult magic. Sophia loved staring into them; like monks who lose themselves in the plasmic dances of flames. They seemed to have a layer of thin liquid covering them; the tear between here and wherever they were going. You could never quite see through because of this distorted stratum; it moved akin to rocks hitting water, with occasional crackles of black lightning that would change the pattern of these ripples. It was all stages of matter but none of them. Regardless of what type of magic created them or where they were going all portals Sophia had seen looked the same. Yenya stepped through the translucent watery-electric threshold vanishing except visage. A few seconds afterwards the edges of the portal came together rapidly. Closing itself so fast that after-image of dark ball-lightning remained in the doorway, but this too was quickly gone. The door slammed and once again the room was slumberous.

" That isn't quite what you fucking said would happen Maaaster" Sophia stretched out the word in cocky disapproval.

"I know, I know. In my defence now I can tell you I voted against testing you." Arthur relented with a softened voice.

" Weeeeird test. All I can remember is that the dream was… draining me... and then…What actually happened!?" Sophia cut her own searching short, demanding come sentence end.

" I already tell you too much but what happened Sophia was you were purposefully scared and cornered and so you performed a spell you shouldn't know, a spell that as far as I'm aware I haven't taught you, a dangerous spell not in any of the libraries but instead hides in my diary" Arthur spoke melodically, as to add a touch of joviality to the chastisement.

" Why do you even scribble into that thing? The whole point of your Grimoire is it can't be read by others. It was the first thing you taught me. I shouldn't have even been able…" The girl stopped herself though Arthur didn't need the pause to be given;

"Not your business my STUDENT. Anyway, one should fully understand the forces they wield before they risk their lives to wield them. Not many are even worthy of that!" Touching that nerve burnt up the remnants of guilt within him; his teacher's mask had now fully returned.

Sophia looked down shameful from the snap but only for half a heartbeat. Predator she was her eyes raised back up. She would not hold her tongue;

"Do the other Master's lie to their students too?" She got braver adding condescension to her tone.

"I'm not sure, do the other students steal from their masters?" He asked flatly. There was no fun left in him.

The girl broke;

"Okay, Okay, I'm sorry, shit, it wasn't even like that. I jokingly mumbled that I needed to know more about your diary to myself but Querf heard and sensing how much I wanted it he shot off and…. I am sorry though.".

Many people would look away after an apology but as vulnerable as she felt Sophia held eye contact with Arthur.

The Man puckered his lips and lowered his brow as if to say 'what have I told you about that creature' but then his face changed, dropping the expression. He looked at the ground and smiled ever so. Sophia gave sigh of relief; no grand reprisal was upon her; continued tutelage meant any kind of punishment did not matter to her. More-so she believed her master saw the humour in the event. However, Arthur's smile was birthed from his own relief, something not often saw by his disciple of 15 months and so unrecognised. Relief that she hadn't entirely chosen to invade his privacy, she hadn't read it all and thankfully did not realise the reason for why it had to exist.

" Come on, I hate this room." As he spoke Arthur gestured his only hand into a thumb pointing over shoulder towards the door. She nodded in understanding.

They walked towards the door next to each other. The man's age slowed him, but he moved proudly, intent-full large striding steps making up for this. She moved in short light-footed steps, many a time, though smaller she could easily outmanoeuvre him. Arthur was more than aware of their differences, and he liked that his pace made her slow from hers. Before they reached the door, he subtly nodded towards it. She took off like rabbit, reaching it, it was many times her size. She had to grasp the handle with both hands to pull the great door too. It swung inward taking her with it.

Arthur passed her straight faced though he found it amusing. Entering the great corridor, he noticed it had turned rose red, which he did not like. It was rarely so definite and opaque in its colour. But he let it leave his mind promptly. Even with such a long corridor he didn't want to squander time. There was no room for fleeting fancy and mild concerns. Bigger things were afoot.   ,

Sophia had rapidly caught up with Arthur, though she hadn't returned to his side but trailed behind him. She couldn't help but have her focus shift to the walls of the many-doored corridor. It was always a mixture of colours or at least a weird shade but currently the brightest red. She swore it could almost talk so what was it saying today. Strangely, it made her think of anger. She retook her mind and pushed the ponder back to common thoughts about the doors she wasn't allowed behind. There was just so many interesting doors. Half a hundred and she had only seen behind a dozen of them. If she could choose only one more to explore, she would struggle. Would it be the beautiful golden jewel encrusted door, or the greenish hairy door; It had so many locks on it and she had never seen a master even glance at it.

Thinking of masters, her own returned to her mind. From behind she saw his hand tighten around his belt as he walked, 'a psychical habitual thing' the blood-witch thought. His belt around his garb could without blood magic become a rigid walking-stick, but this was rare and only seen by Sophia and Yenya briefly after waking from sleep. She reflected on how he hated his age, many of his gowns even hung so low they covered his feet. One never knew which way they were facing or how poised. She heard the non-verbal intonations that meant he was about to speak and began to worry he would notice her only half paying attention. So, she paid no further mind to it all, it wasn't her time yet. Thus, she returned to attentive student mode giving a double skip to catch up reaching his side as he began to speak:

"Do you remember your first magic theory lessons? Explaining, that we resonate with different schools dependent on what symbols and icons we were raised with. That your subconscious, your shadow side grips onto these. This and more are all influencing you when you translate the unseen forces you wield. Manipulating reality takes more than manipulating your outer form." He spoke with strange tonal changes; he was in teacher mode.

"Yeah yeeeah. If I liked singing or moving my ass around instead of art and shit, I wouldn't be a blood-witch and that any person wielding any type of magic can become a great force if they understand themselves." Her response nonchalant but proud.

"Well I lied. Magic is complicated and that book learning refers to the norm. For example, I did not choose the school of blood, I did not even pursue magic. For another, some people have a far more powerful connection with magic than others and can even wield multiple magic's, like Yenya. These people shape the world. Things I've downplayed to you mean more than I let on. Being a student to a master and not a book means you have more than my spells; you have my quirks; my secrets.,. or will." Arthur was rambling, his teacher-mask slipping.

" Err okay." Sophia's perplexedly twisted her face as well as her words.

"I'm part of your magic more than you realise…What I'm trying to say girl, is no matter where your future takes you a little version of me is with you." Arthur used his kindest voice, though it was rusty.

" Oh, I see, but what's going on? You going somewhere? You're rarely soppy. Everyone is being odd I got a bad feeling…" Sophia's increasing tempo and slowing pace indicated she was starting to worry.

So used to being interrupted by her master, now, she ceased when he spoke. His consoling was accompanied by giving her awkward pats on the back;

"Don't sweat, I'll clarify thence you worry. It looks very likely the school will be disbanded and more so than that; Things are about to change…for the worse. Arthur looked away from her before releasing the last of his words.

SHIT. When? Do I go!? Or will I get to finish training with you!?". The witch's tempo grew with her concern.

"I know I'm burdening you with a lot, but we will discuss everything tomorrow. Go talk to your friends about their dream-trials and do not tell them or anyone everything we have spoken about." With this he slowed his own pace and looked intensely into her heterochromatic eyes but as he finished his head turned straight again.

She had been looking back into his old grey eyes so hard, trying to affect him, she hadn't noticed they were coming to the end of the corridor.

The giant door was already open, so she looked ahead to and through the silvery sandstone archway to try see the other students. She couldn't yet; 'they will be standing around the fountain talking'. Which was common, though the extra energy was palpable everywhere. Arthur once again nodded his head to direct her, though now it was encouragement. She left, lingering and bedazzled, not her usual pace. Arthur used sad eyes to watch her trudge away. Her head spun around before reaching the archway, looking back as if to say, 'I still think your hiding something'. Arthur felt the message in her gaze and turned around walking back up the corridor. Towards his home away from home, the celestial door. He felt bad lying to her and about so much more. He did not know if it was: this guilt, the similarity of the approaching, Yenya's obvious words or the girls' devoted eyes. For whatever reason he found himself rubbing his rights arm-stump again but this time thinking back. To all those years ago to when the man he was had this life forced upon him...to the last time a witch was sacrificed...

Chapter 3. Deathly Dawdle

<u>FLASHBACK</u>

His body was so fast back then and magic barely a concern. At least not an internal one. To the tables finest knight if anything it was distasteful and went against God's design. Even the nature-magic of the field workers thorned his mind when he ate their produce…Though bigger, he was a smaller man then. Never seeing the bigger picture, or how each of his choices was a brushstroke painting more than just his future. He relished in success and regardless, what was a greater goal to pursue than vanquishing the realms biggest threats.

His sword hung heavy in his hand, burning his bicep, he refused to have it enchanted.…*He missed that sword, even though it would be useless to the man the centuries had made him*…He struggled to remove dented helm. Though his head no longer rang he had tasted blood since the last battle. It did not matter; the campaign was nearing end anyway. He took deep unobstructed breath to cool himself, summoned and spat the filth from his mouth. Looking up at the strange sky, he knew this was the spot.… *funny how he couldn't remember the landscape entirely, just the poignant*…Black trees surrounded by their dead leaves and a small hill a yonder where sky-fallen lights were hitting sporadically. The knight chuckled at the ease of it. He was great with directions though origin of the dark magic was always atop a hill and hellish creatures always below.

As his view fell back down it was drawn to the obligatory "dark-guards", yet this time was different. His focus was sharper than usual and his gut rumbled dread. It had been a year or so since he had tasted fear but that always went in hand with the unexpected and this was unexpected. Odd even on a quest like this; they wore no armour, showing off unnaturally toned muscles on disproportionate forms. They were pink but with such a strange hue and texture to their skin. As they grew closer, he saw their faces, they were horrific. No noses, no mouths, eyes dripping from a lack of eyelids, they were not human, but did they used to be!? He could not spend more energy discerning the faces further or pondering their beginnings. Outnumbered, like always. Four of them. The three running at him had closed half the distance already. He could not run that fast. The one whom stayed back by the hills bottom seemed twice the size of the others. Without blade focus he would not be facing it…. *even back then he was the thinker, the strategist, the one who could sway the table. That part was him from the start, not given. Arthur was jealous of himself; of a man who didn't know…*

Time to prepare; two wielded axes, one a great sword like himself but black metal and seemingly 9 inches larger. They moved without finesse, more like rambling beasts. This was his indicant. They would use wild sweeping blows; all slashes no lunges. They will attack together but staggered from a lack of coordinated patterns. The fear was pushed down, he had his plan. Excitement in its place as he let only his own world matter to him and not what happened without him. Now at worst he would enter myth with a Valhalla-like end against true evil …*well, now his perspective allowed him to look back and know they were mostly victims. They had their own minds but were birthed by and with ill-intent, more instinct than minded and were closer to doing evil rather than being it…..* The three thundered closer, now 75 meters away. Arthur's hands squeezed around the handle of his weapon tightly, he rose it above his head and held stance.

The first abomination reached him a bound before the others, swinging its axe high and horizontal trying to take the head. Arthur had already knowingly taken knee, the swing missing him, then he rose springlike thrusting sword up. It jutted up through the creature's neck and out the top of its head. He then jumped backwards holding arms bent retrieving his blade forward through the face. He had given it a mouth. The next blow had already been thrown, though it wasn't in Arthur's eye-line until the corpse fell. An axe flying towards his face. He came across right to left with the blade; whilst the momentum parried the axe away it flung the knight off balance and onto the back-foot. It mattered not. He was trained for such things. He used the momentum to drop his body downwards as well as backward, shifting all his bodyweight. Though it felt like it ripped his calf then quad muscles he flung himself forward stabbing the second through the chest. The infernal creature grabbed the blade with both hands and cared not of the impalement. It looked into Arthur's eyes with hate. The silence is what stunned the warrior's reflexes as none were quiet when killed, though he had never faced the mouth-less. As the fiend held tight it guaranteed the knights steel remained within itself and the final attacker reached the handicap-battle with simple plan; it lunged its great-sword without breaking pace. Stabbing its own comrade in the back with enough power to pierce through its entire body and out its front. It carried on, piercing the front of Arthur's battered armour where its point tickled his rib. The man screamed in pain, and he felt the usual warm wetness.

The final brute was stunned with its own success, but the pain had awoken the knight from his dazed concern. He had realised the two swords within meant the second creature was dead standing; it had released the base of his sword. Arthur jumped back then sideways, a well-versed sidestep, retrieving sword and facing the creatures; third left holding up the second. Before it could pull its sword from the back of its companion Arthur put his entirety into a roaring blow. Taking off both heads in one straight-armed sweep, the living one but the dead as well..... *Arthur smiled from the recollection. If not his finest move one of his favourites. Shame it never reached legendary status, like a Yenya deed....*

The bloodied knight fell to knee and hand, barely able to keep his face from kissing dirt. He smiled broadly in celebration for a handful of heartbeats before a fear struck it from his face like a punch. Horrendous high pitch laughter, taunting and screeching; like a bat mated hyena like knives were stabbing the air. 'The fourth! The giant! Why had it not approached? Not attacked!? How had he forgotten?' He raised his head and looked over towards it. It stood where it had. It was guarding the hill and nothing else mattered. It was far more heinous than its predecessors; the bellowing laughter came from its chest! A giant opening nipple to nipple, it opened large enough to eat a man whole and had more teeth than a shark. The abyss within was totally black, no visible-tongue, just darkness with a border of razors. As it met eyes with Arthur the monster stopped laughing bringing the mouth shut, closing its chest but leaving lipped opening; teeth smiling. A warning. It began to clap. Huge, webbed hands clawed and homunculus-like. Arthur knew his chances against this mouth-chest monster were depressing. Fear turned to terror, but he was not just a knight, he was Arthur Palegray, The Knight. The king's own and table sent. The only one left of the 33. He pushed, sitting up onto his shins and took a slow, deep, frame-resetting breath. He began to remove armour, first helmet, then chest-plate. It was too heavy in his tired state and speed was needed. It did not want to fight it wanted to swallow him or bite off his head. It did not even have a weapon. This was a hunt. He got to his feet, checking his dagger was still in its hilt. The clapping stopped but he would not gaze over, his ears would warn him. He carried on until all was removed except wrist guards, for blocking. As he got to his feet, he did his best to push the fire down in his guts and picked up his sword. He stumbled towards the beast dragging sword one handed, its point rustling grass, cutting floor. Everything too heavy, the situation was too heavy, this was his death. 50 feet from reaching the beast he stuck blade into ground, he would get it on the way back. The wishful thinking made him chuckle. The mountain-guard made itself ready, a strange pose. He would bait it but stay away, wait for it to try to devour him; it will use arm assisted leaps with large snapping bites. This is when he would dodge throw his knife into its mouth abyss and head for the top, hoping. He stopped 10 paces from the beast, settled himself enough to enact his plan but before he could finish approach and engage everything starting to shake. Arthur had only heard of earthquakes but somehow, he knew this was not one, it sounded more like the earth was roaring than quaking, A surface origin. The wounded man looked to the top of the mountain knowing times sands were running. All the same the creature demanded his attention as it continued its shrieking laughter and began approaching him. Arthur scuttled back a good distance before forcing himself to stop and take low pose. The creature stopped at the knight's grounded sword.

It clumsily took the blade one handed then easily pulled it from the ground and held it above. Arthur didn't want to believe his eyes but then with deep growls not used to words, it spoke;

"HERE TO EAT, NOT EATEN. NEXT SUM". The mouth closed tight, no smile.

But before Arthur could think, let alone reply the being plunged the sword down through its own head all the way to the hilt. It fell, dead. The man was flabbergasted. Head spinning, ground shaking; He broke out into jog. Passing corpse, he was surprised how easy it was to remove sword; the creature was decaying unnaturally fast. Already gooey. 'Was that where the luck ends', he thought. As he moved his mind pounded as much as his body, right arm dead as he dragged sword upward and upward towards the top of the mound. Soon he could rest it. He spoke aloud to self soothe as he neared the top:

"Better just be a fucking witch up here". He panted the words to himself.

He pondered one last time before pulling himself up the final earth-curl. So many beliefs had been shattered. He needed to be brash and knowing to be a knight. He never knew this pride was so mutable, he wasn't entirely the man he thought he was. Hoisting himself up he took battle pose but was shocked to find nothing but a very small old native woman. Not your usual looking witch. She was sitting in a giant pile of blood making pictures with it and mumbling though. There would be no guilt, he was actually happy at the seeming ease of his final task. However, as he approached her another roar sounded, the loudest yet, it shook the floor wobbling his footing. She didn't open her eyes but stopped mumbling & moving;

"Look for yourself, I may hurt you but I'm not the enemy." Her voice was raspy but somehow sweet, Arthur thought it like honey-oil. As she spoke, she gestured her hand behind her to the far sided ledge.

He approached but past her and looked over the ledge, now he was fear frozen. Petrified. He saw what could make sound enough to rumble the world. He fell to his knees; over side the ledge deep below, burrowed at the mountains core was what could only be described by Arthur as hells gate.... *the old man chuckled at his past self. So naive those thoughts of hell and its doors, he didn't have the words at that time to even verbalise...*Forms that were cousin to fire swirled, crazy and curious lightning danced and rocks tumbled. All of this and more tore open the earth but deeper than stone, somehow deeper than air. An entrance to another plane would be enough to stun a hero but the real horror was what was trying to squeeze through. What would not fit. A creature Arthur could not describe. Mainly as its body consisted of so much, he had never seen, as well as moved within and out of itself, ever changing its shape and number of appendages. The only thing more numerous were its varying mouths. Like a finger in a lake, it currently had what could only be described as its arms reaching through the tear. It rescinded itself but had far from given up. With the haste of a trapped submariner ditching gear for freedom as air was running out it began ripping at itself, taking off parts of itself. Rabidly and furiously cutting and biting. Shearing off limbs and jutting outgrowths as well as the deep slabs of the flesh they sat on. Arthur wondered if it felt pain during this, as it was stringy and black under wound but there was no bleeding. He was glad it had no eyes to see him watching. Then as if it heard his mind, it stopped the struggle and made noise from its smallest mouth; this one different from the low pitch ground-mover but instead so high pitch it made the knights ears hurt. He pulled his head away from the ledge bare his ears bleed, or his eyes. The noise ceased.

" How in heaven am I supposed to fight THAT!" Coughed out the man.

He clambered to feet, leaving sword by ledge and turned walking towards the Witch. He saw now her eyes were open one was red the other blue. She spoke to him in a quick pleading tone:

"Whod've guessed a sister next, lucky really. She wants to eat the world and only I can stop her, but I've not enough left in me to summon the strength needed. I have just enough to…shut the door. I need your strength too. I know your scared but you're a knight, be brave, I can't do it alone, can't stay and go." She walked as she rambled, gently grabbing his arm whilst passing him.

Arthur remained looking where she had stood, shell shocked. He desperately reached for what to say, what to do beyond beg for instruction. He then felt sharp unexpected pain in his right arm. Both in memory and life.

THE PRESENT

Zarros was behind him, squeezing his arm stump. Arthur assumed he must have eavesdropped then got bored watching him daydream in silence. He hated the creep, for so many reasons. For one, He in both lives saved slaves not owned slave armies. He should have reached the celestial room before drifting off, he was getting too old for all the espionage.

" Awwwh didn't know you could be so sweet One-arm." The pirate king mockingly crunched his face to accompany his words.

He had spent too long in his past shoes. Remnants of the knight remained. Arthur spun around to face the 7-foot man, hooking his right foot around the back of Zarros' knee he pulled in with leg whilst striking the self-titled king in the lower chest with a straight strike with his left hand. Although the move was well executed, he was so weak and Zarros so large it did no more than stumble both men back. The Pirate was outraged and with one hand clutched Arthur by neck, lifted then smashed him against wall. Arthur knew it wasn't the rock wall, it didn't hurt enough. It was flat. It was a door, water-glass. The water prison. He didn't care that he could not breathe, he did not struggle.

"YOU LITTLE SHIT!!! You can't win them all old man, what's on offer in life is a couple moments of victory floating on a sea of defeat and that's the lucky ones. I've seen many fall before their time." Zarros' threat started with a frothing anger but ended flat.

Arthur needed to breath. He was back entirely. Nothing woke him like pain. He slipped his hand into his tunic, purposefully cutting it on the sharp middle button then touched the now reddened finger across one of the Sigils burned upon his chest. ESCAPE. Its name was apt. Zarros noticed, and his purple eyes widened but Arthur wasn't pulling a gun he had already fired, and the magic was instant. The large, scarred hand was wretched off him, all fingers bent, and the giant flew backwards in the air as if thrown, hitting the rock wall hard. A normal man would crack then slump; The King of the Pirates stayed on his feet. Instead of attacking with punch or enchanted trinket he glanced his contorted hand and spoke coldly, with a warrior's dominance;

"Whatever you're planning I can smell it, Cassy can smell it. If Yenya votes with us, you better give up the witch. We both know your n' his prison plan aint worth shit. N I don't care, any funny business I'll kill you myself fuck the kick back. Just know I'm fuckin' wathcin'." The smile dancing with his words was ominous.

With this the pirate king took a swig from a beautiful blue tear-drop vial and his whole body darkened, he became translucent then vanished as if he was an ugly gas.

Arthur knew he was invisible, still there, would he hit him? He used his left hand to wipe his brow and turned around, he had changed his mind. No longer would he go through the celestial door but instead the portal door back to the blood-tower. He felt danger was coming earlier than everyone had planned, better try sleep whilst he can.

Chapter 4. Hide Your Headaches

Now deep into the Water-hall, Sophia could tell the group had not noticed her; In their defence the room was huge, heavily ordained with magical memorabilia and she rarely entered a room quietly. The girl was still stumbling slowly, unable to refresh her gait. There was just so much to consider. Her mental monologue fast unlike her steps;

'Can't believe I tried that Nutty spell! It was brutal and how did I manage it, I need to know more.' The train changed tracks.
'As for Arthur…Jeez, so many secrets, bet the rest of that diary would be juicy. Anyway, problems have solutions, secrets don't! Aye that's good I'll say that to him tomorrow'.

It was time to box that away, she wasn't using invisibility and they would notice her soon, she had to put on her mask. Her mind begun to churn to face this next moment; 'Was everyone there?' The girl hadn't looked around to check but instinctively headed to the centre of the hall where the fountain was. The room had transformable seating but that had always been the spot. You could; sit on the ledges, stare at the splendour, even drink from it.

She aimed her scope at the giant structure though resisted being enticed by its liquid performance. The fountain had 5 levels but only the first 2 bases had physical housings to hold the water and this a wondrous black and white marble. The three sections above were masses of water which levitated in disc shapes, each one smaller than the one below. The water cascaded from the top disc down all sections to the bottom; however, the course of the waters odd minded. It didn't only fall straight down but sometimes upward. More-so, streams could move in strange ways, unlike streaming water but in impossible shapes. Some slithered like smoke, spiralling. Others meandered left to right to make geometric steps and some even worked together to rise as helix's, flowing up or down but synchronised. As if this outer shell of varying shapes travelling up and down the fountain was not splendid enough within the actual pools of water, under the surface, further configurations formed. Murky animals with silent watery screams and now and then even more.

As Sophia drifted nearer, she finally saw the group. Closest to her, facing the fountain with his back to her was Taj and his annoying little sister Annaluuk. Her friend seemed to be arguing with the twins opposite him. One hand frantically waving the other holding his sister by the ankle. Anchoring: so, she could lean over the fountains edge. Bringing her face inches from the bottom pool's waters, to watch the shapes. She obviously didn't mind getting wet. Sophia couldn't stop a fantasy form in her mind. One showing how funny it would be for him to let go and let those little legs disappear over-side. It wasn't funny enough to laugh aloud, however. Taj wasn't muscle clad like Candez but now she could see his back and arm muscles at work, Sophia had thought; 'he's stronger than I give him credit for'. He was holding the 9-year-old as if she was nothing, far more interested in the conversation and his animations.

Taj loved bright colours, he was half Leafskin, so was drawn to them. At the moment he wore a light-yellow tunic and green bull-leather trouser. He looked good today. Sometimes his choices were bizarre to her. His height and pale, slightly green skin made any clothing stand out on him.

Though half human he had no physical insecurity, always baring his bodies skin. However, he was more oblivious than showing off and just simply better suited to natures environment than man. Only his lips and nipples were pink. He had well-formed collarbones but very thick and protruding. His forehead and brow were bulging but more brooding than neanderthal. His lips massive but nose tiny, he was a uniquely pretty being. His ears weren't large but pointed out diagonally, almost designed for his hair, to hold it back, waves and waves of golden white hair. It parted at the side and had the quintessential massive quiff fringe. though it was no cheesy bonnet but a large, groomed mane. His cheeks could also rose, but embarrassment came rare. The lightness of his green was his rarest trait though, pale apple. Annaluuk's dark green was more usual of mixed-race lineage, Taj claims his uniqueness is because his parents mirror his ancestor's miracle myth. His cheekbones were high and his jaw smooth, falling into a slightly upturned chin. He often looked pouty because of this when he was only thinking.

His long gold-blonde hair was so unlike Sophia's tailed scruff, instead tied with stone beads and lay elegantly down his back. Sophia was inspired to needle herself; she needed to bathe, she hadn't today. He always made the most of his uniqueness. Pure-blood Leafskin all had dark red hair and usually this was dominant in mixed race pairings too. Even Annaluuk's hair was red, albeit with a thick blonde streak throughout the fringe. She was also a much darker shade of green than Taj, still light for a Leafskin but still obviously mixed race. This had always made Sophia think the child must take after her father more than mother and this the reason for the sibling's differences. She would never tell him but part of her secretly believes she does know how to talk but enjoys her brother being her mouth.

Speaking of mouths and secret thoughts, she didn't know how much she was going to tell him yet; about what happened to her, the spell, the diary and what she had learned about the school's end. It didn't matter, they weren't in private anyway. She would barter for now. The girl fondly recollected Yenya's congratulation.

Next to Taj also with back to Sophia was Pannah or Moon-face as she preferred to call her. She was always close to Taj when Candez wasn't around. Sophia could see Moon-face's bat was tiny right now, the size of a thimble and sleeping on her shoulder. The blood-witch knew this was linked to Pannah's dream-trial. She mused that; 'the olive porker must have been so scared she sucked that familiar dry. But how come she had her familiar and I didn't? Were these dreams self-concocted or tailored? And why am I in such a bad mood!?' Sophia's mind slapped itself, so close now, she found herself double checking the bastard weren't there; he wasn't, thankfully. She had been spotted though; she was basically upon them.

Regardless, as so oft, the blood-witch found herself unable to control her mind; it overswung to compensate for its meanness; it forced her to ruminate on Pannah fully; She was not actually overweight but heavy by design, she was curvy with moons above her hips. Her arms though having the layer found uncouth to women were not unattractive to men but womanly and nurturing. Warmth came with a hug. Her breast was larger than Sophia's needing bra but wide rather than pert. She had a belly but it did not overhang, her skin was entirely unmarked, perfectly dipped in the sun. She wore lots of self-made and family jewellery. She spoke to Taj about it but not often and Sophia would not tell her but she double loved her silvered, meteorite pendent swirl with 7 hanging aquamarine cloudy crystals. It hung from neck to stomach.

Her hair laid on her shoulders and flowed past it but stopped before breast. A beautiful chocolate chestnut brown with lighter brown sun-streaks and flowers always strewn throughout, it was messy and effortless but fit her perfectly. She was always sweeping it out of her face of which was oval with her chin very upturned and small. Her cheeks were massive and her eyes huge to; lovely eyes that looked like you could swim in their blue waters. They showed glee and despair best and wore them most often. Her eyebrows thin and darker than her hair, with her top lip massive but her bottom lip tiny making her mouth small. Her ears were always covered by her hair. The hourglass of her body left her large shoulders hidden by her wider hips. Always red cheeked; that's where her colour broke. Sophia ate her jealousy and her mind returned to the room.

Facing Taj and Pannah and so whom spotted Sophia first was Memtay & Metzu or the snake twins as she and Taj called them. Both had seen her but Memtay, ever angry, was unchanged. Carrying on with quiet yet aggressive yammering at Taj. Metzu, the quiet one, as always grinned that leery smile at her. He tilted head, around Taj and Pannah, as he did so. This let everyone else know she had arrived. Taj jerked his head over-shoulder to see then pulled up his sister. Using his free hand to grab her shoulder he promptly flipped and plopped her ass on the fountain's ledge. Spinning his whole body to face Sophia almost hopping with excitement, he yammered;

"Finally! What took so bloody long!?" His impatience obvious, with his song-ready voice a higher pitch than when resting. His happy hazel eyes eager for her words.

" Well, Master wanted a chat with me, more a telling off really and my trial left me…dawdling." She chose words carefully, not wanting to forget they were in company.

" Ha-ha! What have you done now? Or did he find out you took that book? And did you pass? I think I came first!" Grinning perfect teeth he poked out chest like a hero after speaking.

"Yeah ha, you warned me he'd know. N Yeah-yeah, well I assume so, they were pleased. Can't remember specifically telling me I passed. More like a congrats and we'll talk tomorrow, how come you think you did best? What happened? "Her tone did not give away the dishonesty. Hearing hissing, she knew the twins snake was now looking at her.

She turned to see if she was right, she was, and the reptiles glare intense.

Not only were the twins also eagerly listening but Memtay was now icily squinting his eyes. 'Why was he angry with her?'. The snake that had been wrapped around the twins; under arm and leg, tangling them together had before had its head out of view but now had been invigorated by the new arrival. The giant predators head rose between the twins but higher than both and watched her. She hated that snake.

"Smashed it because of my lucky bad boy" He rose a wiggling wrist showing off a tatty rose-gold bracelet, oblivious to the reptile's rattle.

" What is it?" Metzu inquired.

"And how did it help? I sense no magic in it." Memtay, an enchantment expert, snorted.

"I've never seen you without it," Pannah softly chimed in.

"Or it DO anything." Sophia's mumbled joke ended the barrage and gave Taj smile. Still with sunny disposition he responded proud and loud;

"Awe well you see this bracelet..." As he spoke both girls horned a prolonged sigh, as in unison it caused them to look at each other and share smile which was rare; Sophia half-liked Pannah when Candez wasn't around. They had both heard the story more than once and it was a long one. This did not deter Taj who merely restated.

" This bracelet is a family heirloom. Our most worthless and most priceless item. My dad chuckles at the story but my mother says it was given to her by her father who received it from his mother and so forth back over the last 200 years, maybe more. She says the tale was locked into song to make sure over the generations nobody changed the story. I won't sing it, or the girls will kill me, but my great great gardener knows how many greats, great Grandmother, on the human side, found herself on the run from a murderous man. By time she lost him she herself was lost in the woods. She was not a strong or smart woman but was kind and pretty. On the second day she found a river split in two; one part of the water calm and the other raging, with a small wooden homestead across the water. She fell to her knees in joy and drank deeply from the calm waters, half her battle won. Though tired she knew she could cross but as she went to swim, she heard a noise. Looking up she saw in the raging waters was a peculiar sight." He paused to embellish before continuing;

"A tree had begun to fall, clutching the ledge with root it was suspended above the raging waters. Hanging precariously on a bedraggled branch near the tree top and so above the river was the most beautiful piece of jewellery she had ever seen. A lustrous gold necklace overlain with silver circlets all the way round the chain, they acted as baroque housing; as wrapped underneath were emeralds, diamonds and coloured gems she could not even name. As dangerous as it was and tired as she may have been she had to have it. It would change her life. Having decided she would risk herself for it she walked upriver quickly hence it fall right then. When close however she heard a squeak.

As she looked over-top, now she could see, other side the tree and in the centre of the rages was a squirrel and its three baby pinkies perched upon a branch clinging to a rock. Their branch had fallen from the tree with them on it. Only the rock was keeping them from the rages and their ending. They, like the chain, were seconds from flowing away. She did not have the time or energy to do it all and though her heart and head argued she decided to save the woodland family first. Then try get the jewellery. Granny long jumped in to minimise swimming. Reaching the rock, the squirrel already had its children on its back, and it jumped onto her head whilst she clung to the rock catching breath. When she looked over shoulder, she could see the jewellery was gone and she cried out in disappointment. She swam across to the other side towards the homestead but collapsed upon the bank exhausted. She saw the mother's eyes as she passed out.

When she woke, she found the people in the homestead had taken her to their bed. They were Leafskin. They didn't like humans but enjoyed doing the right thing. Uncommonly all ended up making a great bond with her when rushing her through breakfast; A greyed male squirrel jumped bravely onto the table, delivered her a bracelet, bowed and left. After seeing its crude design; as if made by animals who only half understand humans, wanting to replace something sacrificed, something they only half understood. It was covered in tiny hammer-like marks and instead of a diamond or valuable stone, set in its centre was a regular looking white pebble. She told her soon-to-be friends the tale and they told her this was a great gift for her family and that they would be protected if it was worn. And oh-so-oh it's been handed down to the first-borns and all my kin have lived looong lives. Since my birth I've had it on, I promised my mother I would never take it off until I had child and I never have". Finally finished he gauged his audience.

Annaluuk had rolled her eyes, the Twin's quizzed look was growing impatient, Pannah was listening intently and Sophia wryly smiling.

Seeing this was the collection of faces he hurried;

"So-oh-oh, when they brought me into that dusty mirror room and Cassy patted me to sleep, I must have been gone only a moment. You see, I woke up sitting atop this giant tree, I'm talking mountainous. I'm literally perched at the top of the world. The girls know I hate heights and you couldn't see the floor. So, it was bloody awful, threw up in my mouth a little. Could taste lunch. Might as well of been stuck on the branch I held it that tight and no obvious magic's came to mind even though I can think of loads now. Instead, I was going to climb but when I looked down at my clenched hand to prise it off to begin going down, I saw that I didn't have my bracelet on! I didn't even have a dirty mark; it was if it never existed. This was a huge jolt of reality and whilst I didn't remember fully what was going on I did think 'phew just a dream' and so…I jumped. And I flew… and as I flew upward, I awoke and then it hit me it was a trial and most the masters were laughing. I played it off like I even knew. None of you just… Instantly realised it was a dream." Taj finished speaking quickly but kept pride in his pose.

The snake-twins had both had enough of listening to what they thought drivel. Memtay as usual in joint decisions was the one to speak for them;

"Sophia do you think the masters are lying to us?" The tone was cutthroat, as expected from the students of Zarros. More-so it showed why they were there. Not at the fountain for camaraderie but information and more specifically for the blood-witch.

The witch was surprised, dumbstruck, so Pannah filled the gap;

"Memtay and Metzu have been saying Zarros has been acting weird and they're worried something eldritch is coming". Her tone was confident and without the oft-common anxiety.

Taj's demeanour flipped. He begun spinning his face around looking at each of the students as if he had missed the trick. He didn't see Annaluuk, by his waist chuckling at this.

The twins remained plain faced and facing Sophia. Icy eyes awaiting reaction. Even the snake regarded her with odd patience in its slits. She thought Metzu's eagerness and faux warmth was also lacking, throwing her off further. 'Damn were they being intense'. She wanted to reply instantly, naturally. Her quick mind normally quicker than her opponent. Always fast enough to formulate but the twins were different. They can always tell. Taj thinks she's wrong, but he doesn't tell lies and so doesn't always see it in others, but she thinks they know when someone's dishonest. The girl's half-truth finally came, soft but poised;

"I do think were not being told everything, Arthur's certainly keeping things from me. I don't know what their plan is though." She knew she wasn't really lying here.

Memtay clenched his jaw at this and Metzu discharged humoured snort. The snake tilted its giant head like a confused dog. Metzu took lead of their response, thus the words be civil;

"You never make it simple do you Soph". Metzu chortled with desire now back on his brow.

With this violence had heard enough. He made his noise of disgust; "Eurrayk" and began leaving. Metzu lingered and so the snake always intertwining them was moving to accommodate their disparity, by the time Memtay was 5 paces away just 3 rings of the snake's tail remained around his arm. So, he flashed them all a sucked in lip look of longing and hurriedly turned to catch up.

watching them leave she analysed; they really were very monk-like in how they walked as well as how they held their faces. Though one often loose and one tight; they must have done and rejected some sort of spiritual study. Their differences slight but definitely there.

Metzu's left eye was smaller than his right, the variance not vast but enough to cause him squint and removing pleasantry from his face. His nose also slightly bigger and more crooked. Memtay's head was better shaped with slight less egg-ness making him mildly more attractive. His features were also all slightly closer to his face making him discerning. The longer you looked at them the more different they looked to each other. They were twins only in distance or passing glance or to an eye that didn't care.

Their snake had black patch around its eye giving it a powerful aura and its pattern yellowed closer to its head. Truly a giant snake, though unproportionally long to its thickness, it put those off whom gave extending gazes at the twins.

Regardless, the moment passed, the rooms energy changed and with that the twins were gone.

"What the hell is their problem!?" Taj popped the silence.

" They hate not knowing I reckon. So, anyway, maybe some of us should go looking for answers whilst the masters are busy. I know the key for the forbidden moon-library, I heard when Yenya thought I was out of earshot." Pannah spoke with tease, her confidence had built up over the conversation.

" As if. It's probably a test, where's Candez anyway? Would he like such naughtiness?" As the Witch spoke, she hippo-critically thought; 'She really is two people that one'.

With this the podgy girls face reddened and though she looked as if to speak, instead she stomped her left foot. Turning her back on them before trotting off like a dog-horse, without looking at or saying anything further to anyone.

" She's right about the secrets Soph, Annaluuk's trial seemed weirder than mine, they said to me these dreams are our own creations, but I think they were trying to see if she could be broken to command or something". As he spoke, he looked over shoulder, like a man who felt the gaze of another upon him.

"What-dya mean?" Sophia dropped her head to see Annaluuk, who was clutching Taj whilst partially behind him; he was her shield. The blood-witch did think she seem spooked.

Sophia regarded the girl fleetingly; her colour was what one would imagine of a Leafskin. Not the light green of taj acceptable to human eyes but also neither the very dark marble of a pure blood. Instead, the perfect leaf green, a plant made flesh, the tones soft and blended it was prettier than any foliage. A cute girl though her nose was large, but she would grow into it. She shared taj's protruding collar bones but with an over-slender form closer to her non-human counterparts. Her hair the browned red of an alien bark, not ginger, its own colour; its gold streak sometimes used to tie the flower in her hair so not always visible. No matter of hair style it was wild and uncombed, not tangled but not tamed. Her clothes always so without, often white or grey, not unfeminine it was just her appearance was not her canvass.

" Go on show her what happened" As he spoke, he shunted her forwards from behind him, so she was in front, then crossed his arms less she looks back. Whilst adamant he still smiled. The Witch had only seen Taj truly lose his temper and earthy warmth a few times.

The tiny girl huffed and scrunched face like only a child can then resigned herself. She began a delicate and beautiful act of magic; as a mute she would use her control of nature to paint her story and Taj to narrate. So strong was the child no incantations were needed;

Instead she waved little hands like conducting a water orchestra. A few unselected streams flew from the fountain towards her. Her intent now theirs. The water came towards the girl then swirled around her, engulfing her, then entered the ground at her feet. From the floor things began to grow.

A purple Viola flower promptly grew but its stem and leaves made of water. Then the water-stem became a body and the flower a head. So detailed, its face and form obvious. It was Annaluuk, a tiny floral version. Then bantam spiky brown stems shot up, simultaneously and aggressively. They made a cell around her; she was trapped. Flower-Annaluuk grabbed the bars and fell to her knees. The wooden cage started large but was getting smaller and smaller around her. Then one more flower sprouted, a red and black impala Lilly. It grew larger than its predecessor. Its body also water at first but soon it danced into a terrible form. Devilish indeed. A flower-devil.

It taunted the little girl in the cage; running-leafy hands across the bars, circling the prison as it shrunk. It darkened the ground where it trod. The flower devil started manifesting miniature items. Tiny symbols representing things to mock the girl with. What must be her home and many things Sophia didn't recognise then one she did, Taj. Then the flowers, stems, everything surrounding, wilted instantly and the water bodies collapsed. All magic gone. The blood-witch turned to see Annaluuk whom now was weeping with Taj comforting her.

" She hasn't showed me wholly how it ended yet." He looked at Sophia a certain way and she knew they both didn't need to see more, not really.

The child had broken but did not want to say what offer had worked and how small the cage had got nor any of the incumbent details.

" Either way I'm not quelled. First this. Then what Pannah told me, now you and the twins masters are telling you more than Cassy tells me. I'm thinking we do need another night-out but this one for real." Mischief rife across his face.

As he spoke Sophia saw a glint on his eyes, whilst keen he was still foolhardy, too naive for her to break everything down for him tonight, she was weary.

" No, I'm going to my tower to eat and go to fucking sleep, plus tomorrows gonna be longer than today, trust me." The girl narrowed her eyebrows as she spoke like she was warning a dog.

"Aright, should check on Buzz anyway, what time is the meeting? They said there would be one, but I was so quick they didn't tell me where or when it is Ha." His tone chuckle-some.

 "Be one of those gash letters when we wake up, I reckon." She looked around as she uttered, paranoiac; also feeling eyes in this empty hall.

" Yeah yea, of course." His tone now quietened, he considered things solely and plainly, the fun now visually draining from him.

This thinking was interrupted by Sophia giving him a hug and light peck on the cheek. Hugs were rare, kisses never, thus made both him and his sister take themselves back for a moment. Still, before anything else could be done or said she mumbled "a goodnight, guys" and turned taking her leave. As she scuttled off, she couldn't help but have her thoughts around her friend burn her. The mentation itched in her head until she scratched it: 'Your too trusting Taj, you need to open your eyes. Then again. It's probably better your way. Better to be like him. Dumb, blind but full of love.'

Chapter 5. Risk it & Relax

Her head pounded as she walked away, it seemed to hurt more frequently as the years passed. She knew her friend's eyes were still on her; she could always tell when being watched; well, everyone could but because of her youth her sense for it was sharper than most. For now, she knew both were upon her, it felt like more, though she put this down to weariness from suppressing herself all day. She thought she would be finished come evening, not night. Sophia felt her eyes sinking deeper as the minutes passed. Now was time to recharge. She reached the 4th archway right-side of the water-hall, black sandstone with her symbol above, an hourglass. Well, that's what it looked like to her.

Uncharacteristically, the girl ignored all the marvellous doors of the hall; eyes fixed on the end of the corridor. All she wanted was to get back to the blood spires. To her tower. The Witch didn't notice the glide in her step. She did notice she must have gone faster than her usual pace though. She reached the end of the long corridor in mere moments. A sleeping flight repeatedly broken by woken steps. Though it mattered not to her. She stepped through the portal and felt the all too familiar strange sensation; like the body became an elastic band to be tightened and let go. BOOM.

She was back in the common area. So big and well stacked for something so unused. Chairs, Orbs, Games and more but only she was here or might as well have been. There was Arthur but he only used his tower and the large black door was all she had seen of that. Plus, not that his old ass would notice but she had swiped anything cool for her room anyway. Thinking of which she had finally reached her big blood-red door. The common had other coloured doors leading to unused rooms and towers, she tried to get into the green one once but failed. Funny as the blue door opened; nor locked by key or magic but the stairs and tower were both empty and filled with weird fog. She always thought of the emptiness of the castle when in this room. Sauntering over to her door she spat on it.

It swung itself open. Arthur hated her lock to her tower-room but that made it better. She clambered up the huge stairs like a determined mouse. They were grey stone, each step a giant single cut brick. The walls the same grey stone but made of blocks even bigger than the stairs. Giants must have made this tower she often chortled. She had asked Taj to decorate over the cold emptiness with nature and he really had not disappointed.

The spiralling walls were now entirely covered in a thick layer of leaves, each leaf from a different type of plant. A sea of contrasting greens perfectly blending their disparity into aestheticism. Emerging from this sub-layer, also all the way up the stairs, were hundreds of flowers, beautiful flowers of all kinds and colour. Tulips, roses, lilies but also impossible ones. Bulbs that mixed the colours of flame and tiny purple bells that would only open to show their yellow stamen when she passed them. It truly was beautiful and entirely improved her vibe each time she ascended. Today was no different. As if that wasn't enough, her nature-wall always remained in perfect bloom; never needing a drop of water. At the very top after the final spiral and just before the door-less entrance to her room was a circle of yellow daffodils with 10 black daffodils within; it made a smiley face; she thought it such a cheesy sign-off to such an exquisite space but like oh so much she kept that from him.

She flopped though the entrance into her room; The day had scrambled her egg well and she couldn't think straight. However, the combination of being truly alone in her fortress and the lingering scent of golden swamp rose her past-self had left in the air for her instantly began slowing her cogs. The girl's daily anxieties alleviated like a hole had been put in a bucket. She scanned the room for Querf, mainly the ceiling rafters as he liked to stay high. Not seeing or more pertinently not hearing him she assumed him out or asleep. He often took any opportunity the window or door wasn't charmed to leave but never for long. Sophia wandered how long he'd last without her to feed his addiction.

Her sight transfixed on the far left of the large room and out the giant circular window, which was masterfully cut from the impossibly thick tower-wall with only one barely visible hinge hanging its single panel of thin but immaculate glass. How easily it opened and closed with its tiny glowing knob impressed Sophia and oft had the witch pondering the unknown crafter; she'd concocted many different fantasies of whom made it and how. Even young windows were quick to squeak or ware and very few had a handle so wonderfully masked; a dim yellow glow centre-left the glass, more ambient than eyesore.

It was the only opening to the outside in her tower, but it was lovely and more than adequate. It would be giant even to Zarros, though the girl was glad he wasn't allowed access the blood spires, let alone her tower. When the room was empty it was the first thing she noticed and made her fall in love with the space. It was decided too cold tonight for the balcony though, no matter how alluringly large the moon seemed. She loved the skies but hated the cold. The castle was atop a mountain and so the view was vast, but fuck could it get windy. Far from civilisation she saw no roads, only the private twilight movements of field and forest. A group of bats was marauding with the one leading twice the size of the others. The blood-witch knew it was pork-faces bat collecting magical energies. It'll be three times the normal bats size again come morning Sophia reckoned.

She strolled to the centre of the room flinging clothes off herself until scatter clad, in only undergarment. The clothing she threw hit various areas, mainly the ground. Each garb had only remained still a moment before crawling like bugs towards and then into the wash-chest to the corner of the room. This was due to the sigil she had carved underneath said wash-box. The old blood smeared across it glowed mildly as the spell was active and stopped when the clothes had wriggled to their new home. She paid no notice to its need of top-up. Though ignoring that she did pay notice to her wall of trinkets and scribbles, she always did. Her eyes held longest on the child-drawn picture of two girls and a man at the collages centre. She had expected to be home much earlier and be able to tend her mini menagerie herself, she sighed, dusk was more than upon everyone now.

She strolled over to the wall opposite the window, to the enclosure; which comprised of nine boxes of various sizes; 2 by 3. It took up a good amount of room-space on that side. All were fronted with glass, but each box's other materials varied. Each was strange in its own way as each one uniquely catered for its owner. This made a clashing colour scheme.

Such a strange furnishing it was clearly one she had made herself. The blood sigil below it was already glowing. A large silhouette of a spindly man filled with innumerable stars, more glints to a human eye, was already feeding and watering each animal. In turn tending each specific need. It looked over-shoulder at Sophia dismissively before carrying on. She huffed then hist, the latter of which caused the figure to silently explode; a few glints left clinging to the air and existence, then nothing. It had tended all the boxes except the last three, the bottom row.

The girl opened the first cage, home to her aureate rabbit. It recognised Sophia and joyfully jumped towards her, but she put her hand on its face to stop it; 'he can come out in the morning instead'. She reached into the bag in front of the coop, the one the silhouette had been using, pulling out carrots and an antique fragile-looking water bottle. She chucked the food into the silver trough within and filled the water-bowl, after-which the bottle remained full. A useful relic indeed. She closed the glass. The girl skipped the penultimate box as the animal within was the epitome of no appetite, a desert smoke viper. Sally only ate once a year and never drank. It was easy to tell the day too as that's when she took her most corporeal form. The girl peered within. Light grey-yellowish smoke in the form of a snake glided up the walls and in and out various crystal-hides. She would however let the final box's critter out. It was his turn and the witch tried to be fair, at least most the time. The enclosure though glass fronted was tinted black, the creature not fond of light. The room was dark enough right now, it being night. She gently turned the spiral black-glass nub three times and the front flicked open. Like a shot, a flash of white passed her. Too fast to track it would panic the uninitiated. Sophia though, smiled knowing what she was about to see as she turned.

The animal was flying; however not by wings but oscillating through the space by tail. Now moving slowly, the witch could see her little Penny truly. He was a Yah-matso; Penny had immaculately white hair except for the tips of which were opalescent, and this hair all over. He had a long body with 4 legs reminiscent of a wolf but was much smaller like a cat. The tail was wide and twice the creature's size, the proportions of a squirrel. Like a hairy fin, when it flew the fin moved as if the air was water and made its flight a wonderment to behold. Its head couldn't be further from canine, more like owl. Round with huge also round eyes taking up most its face; cute but darting, always moving. No nose but also no beak, instead a tiny hole; it fed by quickly swooping in, vacuuming up tiny scraps then speeding on its way. Rarely seen, it only swims through air slow like this when at rest, play or mating.

She watched the being stretch it's self out as if yawning then start dancing through the air like only it could. She walked over to the animal-bag and reached in deep. Such a funny bag; it could hold more than its size gave credit. As well as being able to put a delicate item within and kick the bag and it wouldn't break! Still, her favourite thing about it was that one didn't need to even look in it. Just hold what you're wanting in your mind's eye with hand in bag and what your picturing will softly bump into your hand. Well only something put it in before then of course. She often found herself lifted, picturing fanatic items with her hand within; pipe-dreaming by chance they would be real and be in the bag so come to her. She projected what she wanted in her mental space. the bag of dry dusted angleworms. She had it. Turning to the creature who was still flying she started sewing her floor with the dust-worm. First once, then twice, by the third the creature had noticed turned and dove with such speed Sophia's hair moved.

Forthwith it was on the ground sucking up the treats whilst using its back legs to shuffle forward frantically. So funny, as if an anteater which rarely walked found its favourite food and back-legged in excitement. After laughter she turned around and repeated sewing another part of the room. So, Penny used her tail and with a big spring bounded over the girl's head and landed in the new area. After 3 more feeding's the Yah-matso jumped into her chest. Though small the speed made penny like bullet. It took Sophia off feet and onto her ass, she loved it. Cuddling and playing with the mythical beast for only a few minutes before stopping. She knew she must carry on and so said the first word she had since entering the room:

"CHI-CHI". The tone firm, determined.

The creature wanting to please its owner launched into the air, did two loops, extra slowly with excess elegance then shot with its blinding speed into the box. The force causing the door to shut itself and the spiral knob too spun itself three times; locking him in. Even when she broke things the witch didn't care, she was her rarest pet. Today was good, the girl looked around confirming; nothing damaged. Now that was done it was time to really relax and get the tree out. She huffed stopping herself, thinking 'not till she had spoken to Querf - he rarely was gone this long where was the little shit. No matter' she thought further and like Arthur; 'Things are often better when earned.'

Chapter 6. Quizzing Querf

She ambled over to her bed, it levitated there, its ever-present red flame underneath it, fed by sigil-coal. It looked inviting but it wasn't time to crawl into the warm. Beside the bed a floating wooden disc was being used as bedtable. It had 3 books on it and atop them a translucent blackish-red crystal. It was projecting a large floating image in front of the bed, a one-way window to an area of Africa. Currently a graceful gazelle being stalked by a calculating cheetah. Sophia remembered she had rushed out so quickly this morn she had not put it away. She picked up the crystal and the window to Africa dispersed, walking over to the part of the wall with 3 shelves of crystals she placed it in the only gap; strangely all the world-crystals were quartz-like but varying colours. She like many things wished she knew their origin. Her eyes flicked to the emerald-green crystal, New Zealand, that's where she would peek tonight. Before she could pick it up, she heard the all too familiar squeal.

However, the smile fell from her face all too quickly as her head felt a downward strike. Querf had barrelled onto her from the rafters. He wasn't large; a little bigger than a basketball so whilst sitting on her head was fine, he had enough weight to be bruising on her neck with such an impact. The unpleasantness of the shock recoiled her and caused the blood-witch to swat him from her head, hard. it sent him flying across the room. The hand of his big arm hit the floor first, taking the weight, then the powerful arm bent, then straightening it changed his directional-motion and he rose upward high then fell to feet non-phased proclaiming:

"Someone's moooody. Especially since I've done it, your library is in chronological order, alphabetical order and separated into sections by genre then colour.... It took so long I fell asleep after." So pleased was the little gremlin as he spoke, he danced, and he continued to dance when finished speaking. Clearly a dance symbolising his happiness; eager to receive his proportional pleasurable pulse.

The girl watched the little bastard dance, she actually felt bad for him, it was mean of her to give him a task she had no need or interest at all in getting done. He was just annoying this morning and she was anxious about the trial. With everything that has happened today she found herself putting this new lucid light upon her familiar. Could she see him differently too now.

She couldn't. Though much smaller he looked exactly like one of the statues of gargoyles that would sit high atop old Gothic churches. Hence most people's disdain for them. Hitherto there are several differences; He was out of proportion, specifically due to his right arm. It was so much bigger than the rest of him that it dragged along the floor and constituted a quarter of his bodyweight. His other arm not useless but tiny like him, his legs well-muscled. He also didn't have two large horns protruding out either side of the forehead reminiscent of such beasts but instead many different sized horns all over his head. Taking him further from myth they could not really be used as weapons; they were brittle. With what she assumed must not be painful he runs at walls to break them off so often he looked like he did now, with a mass of broken horn stumps. He foolishly thinks it makes them resemble hair. Normally there's an odd outgrowth that he's missed or that has grown back much quicker. This was true even now with a little perfectly formed horn just behind his left earhole. He really was a dull stone-grey too. His eyes though, were pools of grey, many pupils and none. They were water colour constantly moving but always a lens, unknown if they could see visible light, no wonder he gets it wrong the girl mused. In their own way they were dauntingly beautiful.

Querf wasn't complex but aware enough to notion that as well as his horns, he disliked his lack of colour since living in this colourful realm. He has a habit to dress his big arm in colours. Crisp packets, string, scraps of clothing, all sorts. Now he had around 15 clashing colours; mostly in rings jumbled from elbow to wrist. She saw a metallic blue-into-red shredding, a packet. A black bowtie then many worn fabric pieces of varying thickness and lengths from shirts and shorts. Greens, yellows, denims then she noticed a new scrap. A vibrant orange rag closest to the wrist, it was from her new dress. He had cut it up before she'd worn it. She doesn't have many dresses. She snapped, speaking in anger:

"I didn't need the bookcase sorted!" Her blurt venomous.

" What but why! WHY!?" The gremlin stopped dead from dance and used his immense right hand to cover his whole face. His wincing squeal muffled.

" BECAUSE YOU ANNOY ME! You woke me up this morning and

whilst I was gone you've been CUTTING UP MY THINGS". After shouting she quieted but then shouted again. The girl instantly felt bad for the cut her voice inflicted.

Querf's face was too expressive for humanities subtle standards. His eyes could open further and whether fear, anger or happiness it was accentuated by this. His tongue was so large it seemed crammed even in his giant gob. It would often fly from his mouth. He tried to keep this to a minimal. So, it only happened in times of emotion, like this; right now, the blue beast had flicked out his mouth, hit his left eye then flopped down past his lips. Even his reflexive emotional intonations that accompanied these over-expressions were loud and usually jarring. After today's display of disgust, he took off like a shot. He sped towards the mini menagerie whilst singing;

"You're a Bitch, You're a bitch, You're a bitch //
Weren't gonna' wear it Anywaaay 'cuz you're a Bitch." His tone menacing but melody perfect, strange since the tongue remained hanging by his chin, lisping the song.

Sophia knew exactly what he was going to do and now writhing she took off. A second shot. This was a race. Querf was so much faster than he looked and even his tremendous footspeed wasn't his top-speed. He often used his ginormo-arm to launch himself, to become a blur-full wind with no control. He could easily have beaten her, even if she were rested. Luckily for the witch his run was more of a dance; hopping left foot to right foot, the swing of his body accentuated, leprechaun-ic. Thus, she caught up quickly, reaching the little savage a foot or three before he reached the menagerie. Stopping, still raging she swung her whole body into a straight legged swipe, trying to kick him far away. Querf saw it coming, having been kicked before. He had stopped but rolled backwards at the perfect time leaving him unscathed and sitting on his bum behind her. As she missed the unexpected extra momentum took her off her centre of gravity and she fell hard. Right in front of the idiot savant of a familiar. She took sighed breath feigning defeat then lurched a swipe at him, though the Machiavellian ambush failed. He was just too quick and simply performed another back roll, still sitting on his ass facing the witch, he flustered;

"You don't have to lie to me mate. You should have just told me there's nuttin' to do. Much more manageable to wait for a task than to think you're getting a buzz you later realise you're not gonna get. You don't know disappointment. You accepted the pact. It's my biology, you're the only one who can... feed me as you would say." He used the small hand to poke his big tongue back into his mouth; he was in sincere mode.

" Okay I get it, I need something done, I need you to come here" Still angry she spoke with a smile but through gritted teeth. The witch wasn't great at hiding her emotions only her mind.

" Ha! Nice try. For so little I can resist: You don't really want it and sure-zies don't need it. I mean c'mon...It comes with a side of your gonna hurt me." The gremlin now sounding mocking.

She pulled back mildly on the assault, softer yet still hard she spluttered;

"Thought you had superior resiliency, no pain receptor or somethin'!?"

"Yeah hurt my feeeeeelings, cause me perverse esthesis and since WHEN did resilient mean immune?" After this denotation he turned his face slowly to the side as if it were a clock. More and more until it looked uncomfortable, and his chin pointed skyward, this matched perfectly with his pursed lips and crazy brow which grew more pursed and crazier with the ticking of his head.

The girl found this amusing but also valid and the pain was gone to boot. She could not help but soften back to liquid, her composed self again. She stood up slowly and swiped the dust from her bum. The floor was cold without her clothes. She walked towards the silver dressing gown laid across the floating bed, as she did Sophia stirred; both hands cradling her head, partially covering her face, her mumbles inaudible. The habitual compulsion fulfilled by time she reached the bed. Picking up her wyvern-woven garment the girl threw it over herself in a single sleek motion. It was strange at first to wear a scaly garb, but it was too good to not get used too; always making her perfectly warm. Even if she passed out wearing it, she would not wake up sweaty. She jumped, half-turning in the air landing on her ass once again but this time pleasantly on the bed. Which sunk even from her little size; forming a comfortable crevasse. She felt the warmth rising from the magical fire below. The culmination of her creature comforts slowly but surely soothing her, transitioning her mind into one able to sleep.

The witch gazed towards her familiar with smile and tilted head, genuine warmth. Patting her lap, she beckoned him. Querf knew this look and the offer being given, he wasted no time in accepting it. The Gnome did a three-step shuffle-run, like a javelin thrower summoning momentum, then jumped forward and towards the ground. His favourite limb touched floor first, bending from the strain of the movement then with great power he straightened the Goliath-arm which sent him rocketing vertical. Halfway up he spun in a ball rapidly to break the pace as well as move slightly forward, plateauing two feet below the rafters. Sophia saw the height crewed and winced in worry. He landed hard in her lap. This only hurt slightly but had enough umpf to have the girl sink three times deeper into her bed crevasse. Instantaneous the bed balanced itself with blood-witch and perched familiar popping up three inches off the bed then back down. Querf was already furled, eyes shut, face buried. Sophia started to scratch and squeeze him, stopping to massage the big arm once she reached it.

"Okay for real now, I actually do need something important, I need a few questions answered." She spoke in a tone sweet but musky, like honey-oil.

"Ooo real but feels weird, might not work, shit I'm in." The creature spoke into Sophia's lap still unmoved as the fussing continued.

"What's the worst that could happen to the school?" As she queried her familiar the girl was rotating a single finger, tickling the back of his head.

"It could be obliterated by a comet, or perhaps pillaged by an awakened dark-king with all light and power within fashioned into weapons or gifts to bind leaders' minds; To turn the realms strongest shield into a thor…" The familiar spoke with an increase in rising inflections and fastening tone, his response exciting himself until disrupted by interruption;

"No no-no-no, calm-it; worst thing that could happen to th' Masters?" Eagerness had overtaken the warmth in her tone.

"They could all die. Or worst yet be suspended in a timeless vacuity in perpetual pain by means of Divine magic or have their loved and cherished corrupted… These are stupid questions girl." The lower tempo and crumpled nature of his voice indicant of displeasure. He thought she always sacrifices his fun.

"Don't call me that! I'm your master, friend but master. *Sigh*. Okay what's the worst thing that could happen full stop, the worst thing for every living being, especially us students and our masters?" Sophia's words were mildly flustered. Querf was still on her lap facing her but not looking, merely chewed his leg, unaffected by chastisement and ambivalent to her finally formed question.

She took deep breath about to verbalize many things loudly but before the venom left her lips the gremlin pulled up on the leg he was chewing. He yanked it high enough to set him off balance and fall backwards, rolling off her lap. He bounced on the floor rolling backward again, with big-arm clutching both feet he began to rock back and forth smoothly.

"MmmmmM Cahr, you really want this dunn'ya. I can feeeel it, what you plannin' sherlock? Anyway, I surmise your speculation and I got the goods." Still rocking, the menace flashed her a vulturous toothy grin which took up most his face.

"Shame I gotta be satiated before you'll know if your gonna' gaz-out Aye."
The witch spoke smugly, looking down her nose at the impotent runt.

Querf slapped his face with his jumbo-hand, leaving it covering his whole
head he grumbled through it before addressing Sophia flatly;

"So it's story-time for my young ickle master, kay, worst thing that could
happen to materiality and has nearly happened before; stopped by the
magical pivots of this realm last time I heard funnily enough, is …The
hunger could be freed." The imp gave jazz hands to accompany the reveal.
Knowing this is what she wanted to know about, self-evidence being he
remembered blearily she wasn't the first to ask.

" What's the hunger?" The girl was befuddled, it sounded like bullshit but
her gut rumbled like it sometimes did, so she played along.

"Forget you didn't get the visitor here in the beloved realm huh, all sorts
of beliefs; everyone's their own reality's my fave. Well, what's life to you?
What's God?" The familiar looked directly into her eyes as he played the
teacher.

"God is everything, split up and in all life. Experiencing itself infinitely
to power itself with love or something sober pffft. I dunno, I spin out 'bout
the direction of my life and I always snook out of sermons on the great
truths." Sophia broke the eye contact, she hated when she didn't know
something and felt shame at her lack of spiritual interest until now.

The gnomey-teacher ignored her flickers of vulnerability as he wanted to get through his long spiel and see if he would get the treat.

"No. Our God wasn't everything; God was nothing. Well, it was potential. T'was the first and truest thought-system but without time or form, boredom influenced God to change. So, to balance the nothing that's always been the first choice was made. The decision was to do something. God decided to become more. The first ever plan, a complex one creating all with an ordered complexity that cannot be worded. Simply, as far as we understood it; Time was created so things could change state, space was created so things could move, difference through randomisation, etc. All came after these two. The fabric. Then we crossover with your belief, where you miss the point. The truth your missing is not that these billions of life forms and their bloodlines are all 'fuelled by god or whatever' that's important. It's not about experiencing it all at once and having fun that's most important. It was hoped all these pieces of God let's say... immaturities of black and white will return changed by their lives. Coloured. To create a bigger better supreme-divinity who can make a bigger and better reality in the next crunch-birth of creation. To come back more at the risk of being less. Aaaanyway that's the nuanced context, now your able to understand it, the answer to your bloody question lies in how Kyzatsu made it stick. A rubber-band that wanted to neuter itself back to placid origin." Querf's tempo grew as his tirade did, the coming interruption was needed.

" Huh, ky-whatso" The girl only half-understood the lot but that drew a full blank.

"Eeehyeuh. Dialects n sheeit, That's the name the visitor gave and before you ask, he's about to be explained too". The gremlin pushed up, balancing his whole body on his ample fist. Pushing his restlessness through this pose he summoned newfound patience as the end of the task was near. His words came slowly this time but still with a hint of glee.

" Soooo in order for the big-one to make this possible it needed its worst aspect and best aspect to exist in manifested form as the pins holding this good-ol scrawl to the fresh wall. As well as these there's a few other aspects made then left, divine-concentrates and they let's say... patrol. The visitor was all knowledge in form and was to visit everywhere but earth-realm once with teachings. Irrespective the 2 pins are: The good; the Gardner; the one who loves what he's made, fosters it, watches it grow, prying on the subtlest pruning. And the bad; the hunger; the one that wants to be whole again. To end the experiment. To eat all. To snap the band back. Those are the only two in the outermost realm, technically the tenth. Locked away until the end but like all organisations even the... how that book I like would say 'any mainframe can be hacked...'" Finally finished the lesson Querf jumped off his fist and onto feet, little hand clasped within large and looking skyward, awaiting.

Sophia's eyes widened, and she hopped off the bed with enough gusto to soar over her praying brute's head and onto her feet. She used the force to give velocity to her steps, pacing towards the window she sped over her fresh thoughts. Gazing at the moon she suddenly pressed face to glass as she saw a shooting star. After long-pause she expressed the summation of her thoughts aloud not just for her familiar but herself. Now with forehead resting on the glass.

" I think they're all worried the death-cult has a real plan to let out the hunger. Or free some other deadly element of Kyzatsu onto this first plane, our plane, and the rest of the master's want us to be an army but Yenya and Arthur don't think we'll be enough. Or maybe not want us in harm's way…. Aww ". She spun around to face Querf and see if he had response. As her usual confidence in herself was useful but harmful when misplaced. What she saw made her snort.

He couldn't respond. It had worked, counted as a task completed and she did want it quite a bit truth be told, unknown to the need. He laid on his back writhing in pleasure. Tiny growls and foreign noises burping from him. She picked him up and from the force of vibrating she could normally guess the length; this was moderate, he'll be like this for around twenty minutes she assumed. She strolled over towards the foot of her bed where his mini hammock hung off the end. She placed him in it gently, his immense arm hanging out the side as he liked it. The girl liked him best when asleep and this was similar to that. She looked towards her world crystals. With the excitement settling in her belly, she could now feel her tiredness had grown to near exhaustion. Deciding to stick with the crystal she had thrown on the bed when Querf struck her she picked it up and activated it. The air gave rise to a 3x3 meter tear; a one-way window to another place; a beautiful view of a green mountainous region with view of around 20 peoples happenings but she didn't think she would gander through the gap for long.

She was so tired she couldn't even be arsed to trim her midnight fog-tree; which she rarely skipped. Such an oxymoron in form. So hardy when in its hot underground climate but fussy once removed from home. Even so,

Sophia was not so spent as to not lift herself up to breath from its fog. The way it alleviated her mind was in itself magic; to bring in a gas that removes one's own mental fogs. It was soothing like nothing else and was why it is her favourite non-conscious possession. Her prickly mind needed daily pruning just as much as the plant. She hoisted herself up off the bed again with a huff, walking towards the door where a partially obscured vantablack cube sat left side the entrance. Only seen when in the room and looking towards the door. The girl pondered what Yenya would think of her if he knew of her indulgences. Her worries turned to chuckles at the idea Arthur likely wouldn't know what it was. She whipped the bone-needle from her bracelet to prick her finger and returned it in one move, well-practised. Pressing the blood-dropped fingertip to the petite sigil next to the box it began its regular glow. The whole room was plunged into darkness, so dark it made it seem as if before wasn't night anyway. The mild glow of the flyspeck of a sigil gave just enough light to see outlines but the witch was helped by muscle memory and how habitual the activity was for her. She opened the box with one of the keys hanging from her trinket-bracelet. Sophia's right arm wore 4 bracelets; from wrist to elbow they were: her brass one which held the bone needle, the silver which could become a knife by pressing one of its gems, the third, more a band, held 3 keys and the final one a child's decoration she rarely thought about. Not taking the needed key off the bracelet made the turning of it in the lock a funny thing to watch if anyone were. She gently removed the bittie but well-formed shrub from the box.

It was so aged and dried from its nature it would appear dead were it not for its luminous violet core shining out the bark's cracks, giving it its own light. Well groomed, it only had 4 branches, but each impressively expressed like a bonsai; all wrapped around the trunk until the leaved ends that tilted up, so when seen from above it loosely-resembled a star. It was so beautiful it had obviously been loved before and had more than gone through topiary; she wasn't the one whom picked or prepared it, it had previous owners. Like many of her items. A slenderly green smoke also drifted from the cracks, created by its radiant core. This smoke no matter origin swirled around the trunk but looser than the branches, making an atmosphere. The rotating cloud also ignored out-juts to continue to the top of the tree before dropping down to the base and entering the substrate the roots sat it. She wishes she did, but she knew not of the brown rocks it sat in, all she knew is it nourished itself from its own vapours and luminosity. As well as sunlight being toxic to it, it would stunt its productions and eventually kill it. This is how it survives deep underground. Sophia took a deep breath from the plant's smoke, her mouth almost kissing it. The girl lent back and blew out, stumbling back a tickle before breathing in again, deeper this time.

She held it in whilst she put it back in the box, kicking the lid shut she slowly ambled towards the bed. The light returned to the room just as she lay laid on bed, the magic exhausted; small sigil's and small sacrifices having limited effect. As she lay, she felt the familiar effect; the opposite of a room spinning, instead a strong feeling of stillness before breathing out. The green smoke also seemed to hate the light not fillings the room to become less and less until gone but instead coming together in a ball, more condensed and more condensed, greener and greener then when a deep pea it vanished. Before the girl could roll into the secondary effect and enjoy the new thoughts she found her eyelids droop, her neck failing, falling, herself…. asleep.

Sophia could not stay still, she was wet, her ass was wet. She was laying in some sort of liquid so with great effort she forced herself to her feet. As she looked down, she was looking at a puddle, blue. It was the only water she could see, only thing she could see, she looked around and just saw sand, desert everywhere. She strained to readjust her eyes it was so bright, so dry. 'Eh, its hot but not I'm dry already hot, my bums not wet. No time to think gotta survive.' She strained to look further; hurting brow and lid to focus like a telescope, scoping the desert she saw something, a structure. As she trudged towards it, she looked down surprised her feet were not sinking into the sand as expected but instead she walked over it as if it frozen. 'Always getting lost in this bloody castle.' Her chin drifted up without choice, helium-esque; her face found itself viewing the structure again, now closer, though much more so than should be. She could see it was dilapidated ruins. Red-stone pillars surrounding a broken dome. 'Fuck sake, weirdos are gonna be in there, guarantee. No choice but to carry on, already committed.' Reaching the ruins with agenda to climb a pillar for better view opposed to venturing into the humongous dome the girl halted; the wind changed its sound. It didn't say I'm behind you but might as well have and Sophia turned quickly like her shoulder had been tapped.

Nobody was there. But ten steps ahead of her was a stout golden-streaked marble fountain. A giant flat base filled with stunning clear water alive with bubbles from activity. At the heart of the water was a pale boy, young, maybe 8 years old, freckled with many a golden curl. He appeared at first to be drowning. The girl's head tilted at the strange sight. The boy would bob out then above the water to take deep breath before falling back in to struggle underneath before retuning up; perpetual. As she continued to look, due to the speckles of water flying on and off them plus the visage of speed from their movement she saw it; a set of invisible giant wings were attached to the boys back. They beat furiously, there power unable to have him take flight and escape but enough to keep him alive, continuously returning him to air for gulps of life. It was terrible, beautiful, poetic and needed to be stopped. Sophia filled with that angry determination she often filled herself with started to run towards him to dive in. Halfway towards the fountain her body was stopped. She frowned at herself. She had been frozen but knew control had been given back after that moment. A voice echoed so loud it could not be ignored, filling all space but also a whisper the dichotomy possible as it wasn't really outside but inside her; she projected it outward bare it be too much.

" Sorry but you can't".

Sophia softened her anger as she watched. She pondered what could be learned from watching this madness or what may be learned after seeing it. As she chewed deeper, deciding what it symbolises to her or potential others, like Taj, she stopped the cognitive train dead in its tracks. She screamed as hard as she could, not caring if it ripped her throat. One word in response:

"WHY!!!?"

Nothing came out. It stayed silent. As she thunk 'has there been no sound the whole time' her query was answered. She felt herself get hit in the face with a wave of sweet warmth. Not like the blue-beams of sun that had been warming than bombarding her but instead an emotional warmth; like a parent just solved a problem and gave hug to seal the deal.

"You need to be able to truly see this, understand the why before being able to see me. " This came with something similar to sounds she knew, The witch didn't know if it made her think of laughter or crying but her head was started to swirl.

Sophia clasped her face, rubbing, rolling over she swore she heard ol' Privys voice, or was it drums:

"Angers often the son of love Sophia." So comforting that husky vox.

The 17 year old girl pulled the covers to her face, pulling a deeper sleep closer and then over her.

Chapter 7. Saving Soph

Sophia awoke unpleasantly, unnaturally. Propelling up as-if life was blown into an empty balloon; she sat up forthwith with all the haste her toned-stomach could muster. BAWANG. Her ears were being assaulted before her eyes could even focus; she rubbed them frantically and nailed a sleep-mite from the corner of her red eye. Finally, her front-brain was awake and had taken over from autopilot. Instinct replaced with the ability to think. So much to process. Due to its own magic's the window never let sound through, so this continued muffled cacophony must be deafening at source. Baffled, the girl looked towards the giant arch determined for her eyes to battle against dawns first light. She won. They readjusted to see clearly. War. War whilst she slept. She hurriedly rolled over twice and flew out the bed, literally. Querf made a low honking noise as she knelt on him whilst getting up; he had snook in to snuggle like usual but remained kipping as she dashed to the window. The Witches eyes widened at what she saw.

It was hard to see everything; not because of the bordered view a window gives or her refusal to open it but as most the view was taken up by speeding blurs of brown. The girls mind raced: Wow. Giant roots smashing around the castle emanating from its base. Like it had become an octopus throwing an 8-armed tantrum. She now knew how the sound had gotten to her; these towers of nature shattered the ground they hit. Must be the roots of the base tree, Intense. Her mental narration continuing, relentless; she reconsidered how Taj had said he thinks the fabled tree was real. That he had seen the basement door and Cassy had earned it as her familiar, but I shook him off. She furrowed brow at how wrong her past self was with her remark 'your little sis is prob stronger than Cassandra'. Regardless, through the opening and closing gaps of root she could see where the majority struck; they were trying to crush a cloaked figure in the distance. Each strike only caused a flash of white like the spark from stone hitting stone. Everything else a root hit was decimated.

Cassy must be strong and that must be the death cult leader. Sophia saw through flash and root the figure stood with the largest sigil she'd ever seen floating above them; flaming and suspended in the sky it might as well have been a cloud. No. Beside them was a que of people, the downhill cutting her view she dreaded to think how long the que was but as each follower reached the front, they... cut their own throat. Only to fall at the foot of the cloaked figure, who breathed a blue mist off them then kicked the body which rolled to join the pile of discarded. Must be a pile of 50; how could you watch your neighbour in front's fate then still sacrifice yourself. The leader occasionally crouched and wiped hand in the lake of blood she stood amongst. The girl closed her eyes tight at intruding thoughts of her sister. Love and hate. Cognitive dissonance.

Opening eyes and scanning further to the left then right of the main scene she saw 2 portals. From the one to the right giant freaky things were striding out from what Sophia thought must be a horrible place. Zarros and his silver-clad vanguard were fighting them back. Not letting them pass. Well trying. Each invader was bigger than Zarros! Shit: One of the pirate king's men was waist deep within one of their chests! Their bodies are mouths!? Monstrous. His army must be elsewhere. They could only hold the portal on the left, the portal on the right had hordes of pinkish humanoid creatures running out of it; all funnelled to run through another sigil, this one vertical, slimy-green and dripping. So much she hadn't seen. Still with this handicap all couldn't be crushed by root, and many went under-eye, leaving her view, getting into the castle.

So much happening, she had to help. Then a piercing sound. The girl saw it even stunted the vanguard, though not Zarros. He had just jumped off his stallion-size scorpion-mount and slain one of these monsters clean in half with shining sun-gold axe. Sophia's bulb made flash again; Whys Yenya and Arthur not out there? Are they fighting those inside!? Then above the death-cult leader and their piles of death but below the sky-sigil she saw discolouration in the air. No that wasn't colour. What is that? Not a portal... But her mind had no more time to chew.

BOOOOOM *Crack*. 'That's the door', the girl thought, realising she could no longer play observer.

" SOOO-PHIIIAH!!!" Pannah put everything into the scream; so loud and high pitched it just about burrowed through the door and up the spiral.

The witch didn't care what was going on, Loony-Moony wouldn't see her body, all covered in scars and plasters. Not that she was overly shameful just preferred her thinking she may be pure; The girl ran to the clothes that had pre-prepared themselves for her, throwing off the wyvern gown as she ran, she rushed them on; without even gazing the mirror; in less than a minute she was through the doorway and running down the stairs.

Her feet crunched under broken flower; weird, her walls were dead. Shite, no shoes. No time to think. Before even reaching the door, she spat sloppily, it still hit; with the spell broken the entrance swung open as she reached it. Before anything Pannah had grabbed Sophia's wrist and sprayed out;

"Finally, can nothing wake you!?" Accompanying her quick mousey tone was a grasping hand and a look of horror on her face. Sophia had seen her scared so many times but never like this.

"Get-off-me" Like whenever touched, the witches reflex was one of annoyance and along with her spurt she grabbed Pannah's grasping hand at pressure point.

"OWE!" Pannah grabbed her hand looking more shocked than angry.

Released she turned to run back to her room. Sophia momentarily considering the outside of her door was charred. Pannah had failed to break through; 'surely SHE knows something strong enough' the witch pondered as she ascended.

Sophia could feel Pannah chasing, slow but probably as quick as she could. Back in the room well before her she slipped on her shoes and threw on her overarm satchel as Pannah entered the room the blood-witch was already yelling.

"QUUUUEEERRRF!" Sophia's voice was filled with conviction but less loud than Pannah screeches.

Pannah waddled over to Sophia but stopped herself putting her hand on her shoulder for her attention or comfort. The witch was frantically but selectively whizzing around packing her satchel, stopping, repeating. As she was by floating-bed swiping the three books into bag Pannah had forced herself to leave her mind; snapping back in to hurried energy she spoke with as much confidence as she could muster;

"Yenya is dead... he gave Candez instruction, then told him to take Annaluuk and secure a tower. Then, then with last dying breath told me and Taj to get you to Arthur." Tears ran down her face, no longer able to hold the conviction or take the tale further.

The news halted her track. She tightened her eyes, forcing her own tears back into her face she was left not yet ready to turn and face Pannah. Now her plan really had changed. She had to push real fear back. Thoughts of how she would never be in this room again were all that her mind could swim in. Then without agitation those mental waters were drained to leave just one thought and question. The blood-witch turned to face the moon-witch;

"So where's Taj?" Her tone as sharp as her eyes, they easily cut through Pannah.

She popped a squeal, either shocked from the quick turn or query or maybe the trauma, regardless, she closed her eyes tightly rather than answering.

"WHERE'S TAJ PAN?" Though not shouting her voice was loudening with anger.

Her sobs became full tears. The witch thought 'she's become useless. He's not dead, just injured. Yeah injured.' The girl must hold this if she was to be what she had to.

Sophia continued to whiz but now frantic, staggered. Choices being made, sacrifices by the second. Time was of the essence, but she cared not; her animals would not be abandoned. Sophia knew too much of that bitter taste. She stopped at the mini-menagerie and turned bracelet to to knife; She cut the top of her forearm, another long line to join the tally. It was deep but a flesh wound of no matter and no need of dressing yet. Falling to her knees Sophia directed the blood-fall to majority pool, the witch then used the bracelet-knife to scrape into it, forming a reasonably large and complex sigil on the woody-floor. Dinner-plate sized; 3 layers deep.

" You're shitting nuts! I'll secure your common; hurry the fuck up or you might just find me dead." Wiping her now fiery eyes on her sleeve she took for the stairs without looking back or awaiting response. Sophia paused, stunted as Pannah never swore, Sophia didn't think she could even be so blasé. The witch continued; finishing as she lost the sound of Pannah slogging down the stairs.

The sigil breathed in air and breathed out light. The witch placed right palm in the middle of it and down, hard to the ground. When she lifted hand the lucent-blue came with palm, leaving her holding the burning-light version of the sigil by hand. She then slapped the menagerie hard enough for a few of the enclosures to rattle whilst a few others made sorcerous noise. She stepped back leaving the spell tattooed to the structure; The light-sigil grew slowly in size until covering the menagerie entirely before quickly shrinking. The mini menagerie shrunk with it, but the girl did not know how small it would get as she had rushed, a basic no-no of magic. It stopped at the size of an apple and the mark vanished. She sighed in relief before picking it up and gently lowering it into the impossibly light tie-bag aside her before tying said bag onto her; the string tied around the armpit.

"Quueer-Heerrf really need you to hurry uuuuh-up." As she finished her mind cringed; 'Shouldn't have said it like that, the needs pretty big, better bag him quick.' she decided.

She scanned the room with worried eyes but before she found him, she heard him;

"Awh Yeah iz'it." The sound was mocking, the gremlin could smell how much she wanted it.

Before she could triangulate him or bark orders he flew past her, so fast and blurred, by the time she turned he had reached the doorway but now was rolling in a ball. At the first step he held form but flung his ogre-arm out to strike the ground before tucking it back in; sending him bounding into the air before bouncing off the sidewall and down the stairs. he was gone. Not 3 seconds later Sophia heard the bellow up the stairs of Pannah squawking from fright.

'Lords Sake' The blood-witch thought, a rhino as she rumbled down the stairs, reaching the bottom she saw Pannah was in the middle of the common-room clutching hands to chest, watching Querf writhe in the floor in pleasure with confused disgust drawn across her delicate face. Sophia did not break pace. Not wanting to talk about it or apologise she plainly rushed past the moon-witch stuffing the familiar into her satchel bag without stopping. Once snatched-up, Querf instinctively furled into a ball to enjoy the rest of his buzz un-bothered. It made him easier to travel. Before query Sophia was at the entrance to the hallway of doors, in-front the portal she barked;

"You gonna tell me anymore then?" The girl's voice was shrill, however more frustrated than mean.

"No time it may already be too late. Pleeeease. Just let me get you to Arthur." She caught up to Sophia, putting her hand on her before catching a few breaths and continuing;

"But know there are monsters in the castle, they become the magic you

101

use on them. We must be ninjas, we don't want to fight them, I got a few illusions up my sleeve for quick use. Lead way if you want but quietly." Pannah's tone was also frustrated but instead of being the driving emotion it was more of a shard. Nor this or her current intent-full will could veil her fear. She removed her hand and got behind Sophia.

The blood-witch kept her mind's response to herself, thoughts of 'they're not monsters, they're corpses, reanimated then bewitched, well THEY weren't, she knew not of the mouth-chests, they WERE monsters. Pannah must not have seen them yet, no point educating her, she be scared enough. I'm scared too… Taj. She had to stop less her chin wobble. Game-face on gotta be strong.' They stepped through the portal.

Arriving, the path was not empty. Sophia saw at the end of the long many-doored corridor were 30-ish pink-ish corpses, most crawling on belly, some staggering knee to foot. A lot of them were injured. She tilted head so Pannah could see them too. Pannah held breath in silent shock; they could be noticed at any moment. The moon-witch whispered in Sophia's ear so closely it was unpleasant and so soft a susurration she only just heard her;

"Not the worst-ones but we should find an open door anyway." The tremble was almost absent from her voice.

The moon-witch ducked under the blood-witches arm, sneaking past her. She began to try the doors on the left side, the first one was locked. Sophia did not watch her try the next, she had made the choice for both of them. She knew of more than a few open doors, but it was just a hold-up, a defeat.

To win they had to take the shortest path and all who succeed know the taste of risk. Her self-assured cocky qualities arose most often in times of venture, it was her other magic.

She let Pannah keep busy in-front of her, quietly taking one knee Sophia turned bracelet to knife. As quietly as conceivable she scratched a dinner-plate sized sigil into the flooring, thinking; 'even if they become this, we'll be gone'. Pannah had surprisingly found a close open door; the 5th door down, a simple white spruce one. She had the escape ajar and turned back at Sophia only to be plunged into horror as she was preparing magic rather than following her. Pannah glanced over to the mass of mouth-less whom thankfully were fighting amongst themselves due to interest in a door, she had thought they were one-minded. Taking to hand and knee Pannah scurried towards her disobedient ally becoming close enough for quiet communication but Sophia spoke before she could;

"Fuck going the wrong way. Anyway, I'de like seeing them counter this." A half smile cracked her face.

Before she could argue at length the noise of frantic footfall demanded attention, they had been noticed. Both girls looked at them then each other, Sophia dropped the smirk. They were thundering towards them with as much vigour as each had, a staggered pursuit but one that would take just a minute. They moved faster than Sophia thought they would. Both girls injected eagerness into their actions. Pannah grabbed the blood-witch's sleeve to pull her to her feet, pleading, though the witch's head dropped, she continued, unmoveable, earnestly close to completing her spell, she sped up;

"Jus' get behind me and help brace!" Sophia's order was quick, confident and definite.

Pannah flicked one more look to the escape before relenting and jumping behind Sophia. The blood-witch could feel her trembling; pushed up-against her back, at least she understood. 30-40 seconds. Sophia cut her right hand across the palm pretty deep and flicked knife back to bracelet. She squeezed hand to fist over the sigil and her blood started to spill. Feeding it. It was satiated 15 seconds before the attack and Sophia slammed palm to sigil as soon as it illuminated; raising hand as the creatures were at her face. The held spell blasted its magic fiercely. A fast frost that turned in air, freezing then covering all it touched in ice; widening as it left her. It filled the corridors width and overcame the fastest instantly, more so, it became so much ice it engulfed the entire horde in moments, creating a chunked wall. The girl struggled to contain the spells recoil, it pushed her and the moon-witch backwards so hard they slid 5 meters and only just managed to not be taken off feet; mainly due to Pannah's use of her mass.

Closing palm before the whole path was blocked Sophia's spell stopped, leaving the corridor entirely iced except a small gap between the ice and the ceiling. Pannah stood slowly in awe of the witches might. However, Sophia did not notice, she was promptly grabbing her howling-sap salved bandages from satchel pushing past the balled Querf and wrapping them round her hand; they sealed themselves and the wound instantly though they wouldn't increase healing speed. The blood-witch did this then rose, shouting;

"NOW!" It wasn't loud but the noise had a gruff depth that could hold the weight of belief.

Sophia dropped body an inch then took off, a sprint, reaching the wall she did not slow but transferred the momentum to jump upward grabbing the edge. Her hands went cold, her wound hurt as she pulled herself up, a frosty shudder and she continued. This time struggling on ice but still moving well she was brought to a skid at Pannah's tearful decree;

"Sophia, I, I, I can't climb th-that…" She still was breathing heavy from where she had tried and failed.

The blood-witch made a grumble inaudible to her companion. The girl then broke into a half ski/half run back toward Pannah. Seconds being as important as minutes she took to a slide near edge and flew off and over the moon-witch landing on feet; it hurt her ankles as she did not roll. She fell to hand and knee scrambling over to and past a shocked Pannah. Tucking herself into a tight ball, essentially becoming a step the mumbling began;

"Quick, quick, quick." It was repeated like a catchword rather than an order. Sophia just kept thinking; 'How long did they have?'.

The girl noised an "umpf" as Pannah stood on her. She thought 'feels like she weighs two Arthur's or three me'. The moon-witch used the extra height to jump and grab the ledge. She had pulled herself up so slowly Sophia's rescaling left them standing up at the same time. Pannah instantly slipped falling on her ass. Sophia was more unimpressed than tickled. The moon-witch then scrambled up, flicked her hands in odd shape, then rapidly reading her grimoire she took a deep breath and started to sing;

"MoNa MeNon FricTiO SeleNaaaah." Her voice was so high and delicate it brought melody to the jumble.

A few seconds of the beautiful notes and her hands which had been accompanying with shapes went a brilliant white. She crouched, touched her own feet then Sophia's and the white light vanished. Sophia's stare of derogatory confusion dropped when she realised the ice so longer made them slip, she cracked a smile.

"Nice." The commendation made Pannah blush.

They began running level with each other as Sophia matched pace rather than take it to top gear. They only made it a third of the way until the horde started to absorb the magic. The girls footing became uneasy as the ice fell an inch and the remaining 80 percent of the ice began to crack under the surface.

"Pick up the paaaace" Sophia's tone whilst still encouraging started to have its own frost return. This coincided with the blood-witch fastening to full sprint.

Three quarters near the runs end the cracks had reached the surface and dead Arctic-blue hands violently burst through the ice-floor; Savagely swiping, trying to grab anything they could harm. Sophia wasn't affected by Pannah's scream and did not turn head, her eye seeing only the door. Even the threat did not slow her. Jumping and sidestepping the fingered-dangers with ease before leaping off the deteriorating-chunks edge. Landing a bound in front of the door this time she rolled then smoothly stood. Facing back with hand on handle she watched and waited, foot tapping.

She saw Pannah's upper visage appear through her angled view for just a moment before she fell out of view accompanied by shriek. This time Sophia did not curse but wore her determined brow, turning bracelet to knife she approached the ledge. Yet before she could cut herself, she heard the singing and seconds after Pannah clumsily came over the edge and landed crumpled on the floor. Returning knife to bracelet the girl went to help her. Pulling her up she saw the moon-witch's ankle was badly frostbitten and blooded. 'It must be painful'. She flashed Sophia a smile of which the blood-witch could see was forced and they both struggled to the door. Opening the giant black-oak door they slipped through the gap before letting it shut. They stood both breathing heavily leaning against the closed door, thick and big enough to fill the archway both silently assumed it would take a while for the now icy-evil to pierce it.

Sophia's noggin' flashed through the castle, its layout was peculiar; The octagonal water-hall they were in with the four many doored hallways was underground. Most the castle hidden with only tip showing. Leaving it looking half normal from the outside, concealing the truth, an iceberg. This the first of an unknown number of floor levels; students weren't allowed down past this level. She'd only been brave enough to venture a couple floors below this one. Her mind hurt with thoughts of Taj as it raced farther and how his story must have been true. He claimed he's seen near the bottom when following Cass. Regardless, it must get even bigger the further down you go if there's a tree that big down there. The blood-witch swallowed her emotions.

North-East of the fountain; centre of the water-hall, so it could run through the centre of the room above, stood an imposing white marble pillar holding a staircase within. This went all the way through the castle up as well as down. The floor directly above them was the entrance hall, where the main breach was. They had to get through this room and to the top of the staircase, to the guard tower. One room, one staircase, but did the main battle get funnelled down here or stay in the entrance hall; it would help if Pan could squawk out what's around the corner.

On cue Pannah moved, breaking Sophia's internal monologue. Though in the water-hall the girls weren't in the open but instead tucked in a continuation of the hallway, a small walled space of a few steps or so. Pannah had her back to wall, a spy slowly creeping.

Near edge the moon-witch stopped, unwilling to poke head around instead she looked back at Sophia before slipping her hand into her pocket. Retrieving a small white luminous orb, a spell she had already prepared. She threw the ball to the blood-witch who caught it one-handed looking puzzled. Pannah gestured to roll it which Sophia did. It spun a few turns across the floor before splitting. The balls then became perfect illusions of the two girls but made of the white light. It was only for a moment as they were then filled with the colours of life, becoming perfect copies. As the misdirection's walked out of view girls both listened intently. The blood-witch kept it to herself but found the quality of these copies rather impressive, illusions not being her forte. After half-minute the silence remained and so Pannah gave Sophia, who had joined her against wall, a thumbs up. They crept around the corner together. They both were not prepared for what they saw.

They could see the untouched fountain at centre but as they crept out into the open, they saw the room in full, it was trashed. Nigh all seating and tables obliterated so splinters strew the floor amongst chunks of wall and marble. So many magical items either gone or shattered. Blood smeared and splattered across all. The decorative gold gilded heads and floral under-swirls that lined the upper walls of the building which before gave the room an affluent elegance, like a theatre, now gave a spooky dilapidated energy instead. Some were no longer there, others damaged, missing noses and others fully intact. It was half a crime scene.

The incredibly thick walls were cracked, some so large and long they let light all the way through. The girls walked extra slow to allow for Pannah's injury but also out of fear. Akin to prey sneaking through the predators grass they stayed shoulder-to-shoulder. Sophia's eyes gulped in at every element of the room trying to work out what had happened. As they slowly went towards the fountain Sophia whispered whilst stepping over the silver head of a shattered boar statue;

"Was this you'lot? Or Yenya?" The girl did not face her but kept looking around whilst speaking.

" Shhh." The moon-witches interruption aggravated.

Before her own anger took over and have her snap back, she noticed Pannah wasn't just staying aware but more-so looking for something. The blood-witch sensed she was somehow worried about something specific. So instead of battle-scanning she joined the moon-witch. She quickly found herself looking directly up. What she saw hurt deeper than her wounds ever could. The girl screamed a curdling denial a visceral reflex that caused Pannah to hop in shock. It was Taj. He looked dead. Hung by the ceiling by vines that came from cracks in the walls and a hole above him. He was strung up a prize. His face was blue as they were tightest around his neck and his clothes ripped, his hair streaked with blood.

" YOU LEFT HIM!? Is-he-dying? He-might-be-alive. If-we-have-the-body-we-could." The girl yelled the former at her companion before mumbling the latter to herself, eyes to ground.

" No Stop, stop, it's a trap, we need to go." Her head was jerking left to right as she shook Sophia, trying to get her back.

"Didn't even get his bracelet. It. Uh. Did you even know him? With that we could…" She cut herself off and instead looked up at the moon-witch. Her hurt couldn't be kept in and so crystallised. The formed tears fell from both red and blue eyes.

KYYEEEEEEEEERREEEE

The noise so strange sand loud it was enough to shock both girls to their senses. Both looked up again and Taj was gone. They carried on. Pannah hobbling, Sophia shell-shocked, both slow. Reaching fountain, they both started drinking from it, to quench nerves for one, dry mouth the other. Mere seconds passed before both girls bleat in fear as the unnatural noise found them.

Out of the wall's cracks, as well as the hole that ate Taj, vines started to crawl and creep. They were not normal vines though; they were like nothing Sophia had seen. They were vine-creatures; the mouth-less corpses absorbed Taj's magic and were now vines in the shape of man. It made sense Sophia thought, 'vines are always his go to, or were... NO still are'. Her sorrow stopped her focusing. They had faces and arms and hands but now only reminiscent, most of their form far closer to vegetation. They didn't move like normal plants either. They were as if lighting was chained, slowed down. All would be still then jerk together in odd way but each towards the girls, crossing over one another they cared not of entanglement. Their hands were the most dangerous having no obvious heads but instead mouth-less faces morphing and distorting underneath their leafy-skin. Soon they would envelope the room or at least reach the witches, of which they seemingly yearned with their entirety to do so.

As well as this new assault, it was the same moment the icy door far behind them shattered with loud screeching-blow. Pannah looked back to see their old assailant's new assault had begun. The descending icy horde were slower than ever but now whatever they moved over froze. Sophie didn't turn-neck. She knew what was happening, her eye was on the goal. What she didn't know is Querf had goal of his own. As they hurried towards the staircase-pillar a thunder emanating from within echoed down to them. Stumbling to a halt their haste died. Truly surrounded. Any moment it could, it would, be over. The gouges in the wall deepened as more of the vines jolted into the room. The tiny hope Pannah had been grasping shattered, she fell to her knees, she had given up.

" No mouths, so what was that noise?" Sophia cursorily mumbled, stood with eyes glazed over. She knew the futility of it all, but it didn't faze her like it should have.

" This is all YOUR fault!!!" Pannah's voice broke mid bark. Her eyes looked up and stared into Sophia's filled with so much feeling.

"My fault!? Tell me how YOU left him to die, hmn." The assumed retort rhetoric and venomous. The girl's eyes refocused. The pride in her veins always made her blood acidic.

"You don't know. He demanded it! And I... *sigh*... As if it matters now." Still looking at the ground she began to weep to give her tears company.

The girls turmoil had already turned to anger but with this it compounded, hardening. The witch hated everything, hating all these grotesque things most of all. The blood-witch crouched next to Pannah, hand on shoulder she addressed her;

"Shut up, well don't. Sing. Stay alive but keep everything off us for as long as you can." The blood-witch spoke quickly and clearly but Pannah didn't respond.

" Pan, you're a moon-witch…Right?" Her conflicting eyes peered over the threats reasoning they really did not have long left. They were about to get shredded.

" Right." The moon-witch looked up with a fleck of mettle burning in her eyes. She stood up wiping her wet face with her sleeve before rubbing her hands together determinedly and beginning to sing.

Now Sophia forced a smile; it wasn't she was without warm, but her game-face was too firmly stuck-on. The blood-witch stayed crouching, beginning one of the most complex sigils she knew; 5 foot, 3 concentric forms. She didn't need grimoire; Arthur had let her practise this one longer and more than requisite. Especially since it had such a double cost. The training it came after, that it complimented, may hold the answer. It was these lessons she noticed Arthur smiled most. Her mind moved even faster than her hands. The bracelet-knife stubborn on the fancy-floor. Perturb prickled her; 'just woke up, already knackered but big problems need big solutions which…cost. Plus, they can't absorb a change to myself''.

The moon-witch was deep into her song, this one long and operatic. Her hands already beginning to glow with bright magical moonlight. However, Pannah had not come to the same epiphany as her comrade. She had gathered enough energies to start her defence. She would be so much quicker and more powerful if Squeaky was here. First, she dealt with what scared her most, the vine-creatures, using one of the things from her nightmares.

Hands rising high whilst the song was reaching its highest pitch then pointing skyward come crescendo. As the final note broke her hands started manifesting and firing hundreds of giant moths. She spun and they relentlessly blanketed the above, they started weaving silvery cocoons with incredible swiftness. Some around themselves to make points of strength, others around vine-men. Yet, even a war of attrition with erratic soldiers was no more than annoyance. To help their struggle the moon-witch drained her hands, putting the rest of the white energy into one large ball she threw up. As it rose it divided becoming 5 cat-sized flying squirrels, however being oversize did not slow them. They bounded off ornament-heads and the wall and between the vines, biting thin bits and clawing, blinding any eye in sight. These eyes would just emerge elsewhere on each plant though. The moon-witch only took a few small breaths and one large before beginning her next song, this one guttural with many pauses.

The blood-witch was still scratching away having completed the outer and most complex part of the sigil. She tried to focus entirely but her mind could not help but have her hear Pannah. She knew something dog-ish was coming from such a song. She dared not look though as the sands were falling too quick as is.

The moon-witch was gyrating hips, whirling and crossing over hands with sharp gestures. The last low note which sounded ridiculous from such a bountiful voice was held whilst her white hands smacked the floor repeatedly. On the fifth smack as she raised them, they drained of colour, creating a monumental-sized wolf. She fell to her knees to watch her work tired but still not done she had one more song. The silver-wolf already knew its job and had leapt behind the girls, protectively prowling towards the frozen-corpses. Reaching them, it lowered head and growled with enough force to move hair. Even such raw power did not intimidate. The one closet to it leapt on its right leg. Barking, it ripped the clinger in half and as it discarded the mouthed piece with force the whole throng charged the wolf. Some clawing at it, others anchored the beast's feet but most jumped on top of the canine-defender. It shook furiously, flinging many off before crunching down on those on its legs, mangling three with one bite. However, it wasn't enough. The corpses shook off jumped back on and the brute begun to wince in pain from the increasing cold. Pannah still not worried stood at the same time the wolf split and then split again becoming a pack which; freed it, refreshed the frost-burns and confused the horde. The fighting continued.

The moon-witch begun singing. This final one a throat-song; Inuit-ish, long extended notes. She held back discomfort to make herself an instrument, a blackened steppe. The gestures accompanying were slow and sweeping. Extended limb; resembling rain with the hands and dizzying head pendulums representing mental weathers. Quicker than the last song her hands flooded with the same white alas this one dimmer than the last. She threw herself forward on to knees, song complete. Her arms straight laid upon the ground, hands pointing over towards the spiral-staircase. The light left her hands and travelled across the floor creating a shimmer. Then as if leaving water, a humongous moose with uncomfortably large horns stepped up and over three ascending steps came out of the ground.

It blocked the way just as the grim grotesquery's reached it. Unrelenting pink mouth-less clogging the bottom of the stairs. The moose upon contact sliding back an inch but regaining the ground immediately, as it did it gave roar. A few of the quickest had made it past and were ignored by the moose and ignored it. Even with this, the plan had worked far better than it should have. 'How fast had she had been singing? Had something on the stairs slowed them?' Pannah could ponder no more. No energy to help, she collapsed defenceless. Sofia was too entranced to see. The stray pinks reached Pannah, the first kicking her with all its force; she slid back, clutching her stomach. She moaned but did not whimper. Then one of her wolves jumped over her and fought the two. Then another joined; the pack had now split into 4 medium and 8 small wolves. Pannah slogged to foot, swinging the ball weapon from her sleeve she staggered one of the pink mouth-less off her wolf. Then began to sing. What escaped the young woman's awareness was no matter how much she or her forest-fighters were pushing past their limits it mattered no longer. They were starting to be absorbed.

The vine-men had fully absorbed the moths and squirrels. They now were thorned and were entirely covered in tiny black eyes. Now they did not jerk, they moved with smooth-will and they wanted Sophia. The gelid swarm behind the blood-witch had entirely eaten the big wolves and most the small. They were no longer slow with legs haired and more muscled. Their hands now jaws. The frozen beasts rushed towards Sophia. She was glancing the moose shrinking before watching Pannah and the remaining wolves struggling. As those without magic were quickest to absorb it the moose was soon sucked into nothingness and now the pinks were browner with cervid horns. Now much faster too, the moose-men all deciding to take the moment to be prepared and all fully changed for the charge towards Sophia. All defences were gone but they had done their job. Sophia was long ready.

So confident she was smiling Sophia had already activated the smaller of the sigils and was in her right hand, holding a blood-sword. Razor thin with huge face and its length enormous. It was three-quarters the size of the girl, though she was unaffected by this, it was weightless. She raised her right arm straight pointing the blade away from herself and towards her moose-opponents, hoping the half-bluff would delay them. She had already poked a hole in her left palm and with arm by side the wound was streaming, dumping blood onto the giant second sigil. Waiting, she started to purvey. Pannah was still singing but now one wolf-corpse held the last injured wolf down draining and assimilating it until gone. The other about to punch the moon-witch again. Her face was bruised. Her hands were not ready, not white. So, she took the blow, though still singing she dropped the ball-weapon.

Sophia felt pain in her right arm. Making her look down, she saw the first vine had her and was wrapping around her right bicep. More from above would soon join. It's thorns cutting deeper and deeper as it tightened and spread. Then the blood drenched sigil set ablaze. Less than a second it burned bright, an achromatic grey before the blood-witch angrily stomped on it. It felt like her leg had been yanked by the bone. Instead of seizing up, well-practised, she knew what to do and took deep breath. The same magic then took all speed from the room and its beings and gave it to Sophia, though she had to hold it in. It was not the case, but it felt to the girl as if time was frozen, everything still as her skin burned. Steaming as if it had been plunged from the cold into the hot or perhaps vice versa. 'MOVE'. The girl flipped wrist, rotating blade, the tip above her shoulder severing the now stationary vine as it were nothing. She slung off the scrap, it went through air so slowly, it was floating, though if gently prodded through space. Then bringing the blade end upright and handle towards chest she held the whole blade tight to shoulder, perpendicular. The warrior-witch lightly lay her undressed injured-left around the handle too. Classic knight.

From this stance she dashed towards the staircase but moving was a strange sensation as if every angle, every piece of body had to push, like moving in jelly. Yet the power was immense, after just three steps she jumped launching herself forward she flew as if she too were in outer space. Her momentum did not diminish. Carrying on until colliding with the group of cervid-creeps who were frozen mid charge. She severed through many with skilled poise before using right foot, which hit one of the steps, to jump back out the stair-pillars doorway. All whilst sweeping a roaring blow fully circling repeatedly around her head but each angle aimed. Still Enraged all adversary were Taj's killer and the girl removed every head that wasn't on an abeyant mutilated body. The same impulses then rocketing her through the doorway and out the staircase, foot finding ground she braced and spun.

The hurt not yet unbearable she saw eyed vines about to take Pannah's neck from behind were everything not slowed. The girl gave half-second to see Pannah differently. 'Her suspended singing against the beating is kind of admirable......too hard on her, she did well, and it wasn't her fault nobody heard the music only she could dance too.'

Her thoughts drank, the blood-witch launched up and right as if gravity were bantam and kicked off the wall; ahorse horizontal across the room she cut through the creatures' vine after vine. Dodging some, entangling within and slashing to release herself from others, the witch used some to move, before cutting them too. She kicked off the next wall when reaching it and then the next wall; picking up faux speed; a bouncing ball she was everywhere and all. Her own dance. When well above Pannah she grabbed a thick vine at its base to stop herself before cutting it too. Then kicking off from the ceiling she shot towards the moon-witch and the ground. Once she released the room it would rain the vine-men.

As she landed it hurt ankles, she transferred the feeling into more rage. She chopped the canine-assailant beating Pannah clean in half before bringing the blood-blade to waist. Right hand crossing the body, weapon pointing behind as if a tail. A sweeping samurai stance. Lowering body and shooting forward she swept diagonally up and across with blood-sword to cut the other in half, not stopping she performed the same move but reflected. Left over right a multitude of strikes, increasing in speed with each until the girl screamed inside and became a blur. Each sword-strike slicing all without resistance, entirely unencumbered it shredded the other corpse to unrecognisable ribbons, exploding but suspended in place. Only one threat remained but her time was nearly up, it now hurt badly. Her vision narrowed from the sides with fainting-white and the compulsion to breath in inebriated her mind, her skin still steamed but felt like it bubbled. She had held the electric and it had rippled over her for far longer than ever before, yet, she still had one round left.

Control of herself was fleeting, the witch was becoming the girl, wrath readily becoming despair. She lifted the huge-sword high overhead, tip skyward, a barbaric pose indeed. The hairy arctic horde was slowed to an almost stop like the others, but their speed made them slightly faster; Sophia found the slow-motion attack quite captivating. However, it made no difference, she acted with just fumes left for fuel. She ran through the pack sloppily slashing and bearing down as if the blade was a hammer. So haphazard was she becoming some of the downward blows hit flat facing and crunched form instead of separating it. She forgot all Arthur's lessons on the sword. A berserker, one recoil even causing her to hit herself in the face with the blades edge, though a blood-sword cannot hurt its summoner. Not very painful to make and long lasting she used it often but usually for intimidation, this was the first time she had killed with it.

The neglect also meant several body parts were sent heavenward in the pulling up of her weapon, causing them to rise relatively fast in many directions, a medium float. The scene truly was crazy from her perspective but was only going to loom stranger when the room caught up with itself. The girl had to stop now if her perspective was to continue. She had no choice but to hope all those still un-living were too maimed to move. The girl breathed out the pain and the power. No longer able to control the room or herself she clumsily stumbled, skidding along the floor and stopping near Pannah.

Time seemed to seize itself back, its flow continued normally. Motion no longer stacked within just one. The bestial vines rained in pieces; their eyes wide from what must be shock. Both corpse-groups of wolf and moose also showed what had been done to them, all in unison. Blood splattered and spurted in many directions. Peculiar pops and battered bangs all fought to be heard. Pannah saw her halved assaulter in front of her reveal its injury, splitting; its left fell one way down, its right the other. The gap also revealing to her the demented disintegration of the other. Gob smacked she slowly turned around, her eyes found Sophia laying just behind her, dented; breathing much heavier than she was herself. She thought it was if she had just emerged after being trapped in a deep lake. So shocked was the moon-witch she did not act with her altruistic reflex but instead just mumbled down at the witch-pile;

"You really are …. "Her voice frogged, Pannah either couldn't find the word amongst her fatigued-fog or wasn't comfortable spewing it, regardless, unfinished she collapsed right next to Sophia. Whom had turned her head and noticed only one of her allies' fingers was white from the fruitless song. The girls both lay in near silence both again trying to catch breath, like at the entrance, though this time anxiety was substituted by relief.

After a couple more lung-fulls Sophia yanked her neck up, catapulting her chin on to chest.

"You're welcome, babe." Her head smacked back down hard once it had spoken.

As much as her opinion of porker was changing that did not mean the witch wanted to know what her and fucking Candez think of her. Not wanting her to find the word she tried to reach the next moment, so looking to get a laugh she continued;

"Bet your glad you didn't just fly off and leave me here aye. I bet the rest think were dead, huh?" Joviality accented the girl's voice.

The young woman didn't respond so Sophia cordially tried again;

"Pan?" She held the note of her name as if waking a sleeper.

Sophia sensed the girl wasn't hearing her and saw the colour of triumph was draining from her face. It was struck from the blood-witch too once she saw what Pan did. The bits were still moving. Sophia's mind nettled; 'How strong was the fucking magic cast on them'. Fragmented bloody limbs shook on the floor. Hands, claws, paws, all crawled towards larger chunks like torsos. Every eye still full of hatred. Even small vine segments rolled. Any and all evil still able was going to the middle of the room. Sophia's minds-eye could see what was coming; 'looks like they're going to merge into one amalgamative colossal horror. Going to be stronger and scarier than they were whilst we're spent.'

" Okay Pan lets go" Sophia spoke before she moved.

So tired her little stomach it only about lifted her up, her arms were heavy too. She took the bandages from arm and wrapped it round her palm wound to save time, it would continue to bleed now the magic was at rest. Her legs struggled to follow suit. Sophia felt a tug of the blood-drenched sleeve; It was Pannah trying to help her up. The girl took one look back and she allowed the help. They stumbled and scraped to the stairs, ascending them they both mutely worried there would be more trouble before reaching everyone. Their differences were obvious but similarities subtle.

They saw steely heavy roots were tangling with each other blocking the few doors, doorways and holes. Amongst these roots, at their centre, mostly covered also hung sun-fire chains. Shining uncomfortably bright each spell consisted of two glowing lines crossing each other to make an X. Sophia's mind spat its analysis to itself; 'Candez helped reinforce their path. Surely, they'd worry about those being absorbed... What would that even do!?' Sight of a single sunflower at centre of the roots at one of the doorways brought her sadly back to the world. She realised the cracks amongst the pillar-wall were terrifying Pannah, the lofty breathing and head scanning slowing their already snail pace. It was assumed the moon-witch was uneasy, worried more vine-creatures remained hidden within ready to strike or even worse root-men. Sophia saw this fear and though they were further than two thirds the way up, thought it a prudent time to apologise.

" Pan... I'm sorry about what I said to you, Taj cared about you, a lot, and in a way, I wish he did for me and sometimes I... Well anyway he would hate me for what I said, I am sorry for that." The girls stuttered and staggered over herself, stripped to a girl her age, without her confident conviction she vented whilst not looking at Pannah.

" Gah, ha, I wish. It's you he loved it was obvious." So shocked was she, the tired usually shy young woman had snigger drench her tone.

"Nooo don't be stupid, we're friends... Were friends. Anyway, can you talk about it yet? Was he definitely definitely dead?" The girls felt her face redden but hope it wasn't as prominent as it felt, she spoke quickly turning the subject on its head.

Her shoulders seized tight, and she removed her arm from around Sophia to grab herself. Watery guilt filled her eyes removing the mirthful derision from her.

"I I I do not know! and your wrong…his last words to me weren't regretful or about himself, his sister, nothing else but…. Save Soph.".

Chapter 8. One Place Left To Run

They moved without communicating and no longer holding each other for the rest of the rise. Not to keep pace, not due to what they had just peered through the final hole but as Sophia was still reeling from the conversational-bomb Pannah dropped. Whom decided it best to reflect the reticence. Reaching the top, the blood-witch gave shocked puff to see the magically reinforced door to the watchtower was destroyed. The top entrancing wall decimated. All morning the girl had been repeatedly humbled to realise she did not know it all. Already swimming her mind dived deeper, collecting more and more questions;

'What could break it? Arthur? But why? *Noetic gasp* The cult leader? Why else would they leave it open? 'N it's so bright in'ere.'

Some of the answers revealed themselves. Blocking the way was something far more puissant than the door. It stopped them all the same. Annaluuk. Pursed lip, clenched jaw with eyes puffy from a saddened madness only a pre-teen child could wear, though unlike your normal little girl this one's eyes bled plasma. Even her little outfit was battle-worn. Today's flower in her hair was a rose but its original colour unknown. It had been flash-burned, now a hardened blackened ash in her hair. She was quite the sight and Sophia worried about how much she knew, 'no more than half, even I didn't know it all'. After breaking eye contact, she scanned the young-un foot up;

Be it her visage or form she occasionally distorted from the sheer voltage rippling across her skin. The child of nature's breath steamed, and that steam had tiny ball lightning crackling within. It flickered off all of her but she discharged most from her shins and feet into the ground; she was a conduit for the ambient electrical charge. 'It wasn't hurting her. Or didn't appear to be.' The child's eyes were storms. Sophia nodded at her then dropped head passing, not wanting to show her hand, not wanting her to read her. As a mute she often didn't need someone's words. The blood-witch had no time to feel for her she was struggling locking her own emotions in as is. There was also a root around her left leg going straight into and through the stone floor. 'She was the last defence for us. So many would be eradicated by such a powerful magic before absorbing it, and by time they did it would probably all be over anyway. Finally, some answers.' She picked up the pace. Not looking back at Annaluuk or Pannah she took the final two steps and out into the moderate sized room for one of its uses. The scene was…Astounding.

The usually pristinely kept spruce bookcases, seats and walled ariel-weapons had been hastily moved or destroyed; woodchips scattered the ground. Many timeless tombs may as well have been bugs the way their pages were left to scuttle the floor. The many miniature flags each crested with those who came before remained. There were only two windows, they were giant and either side of the room. The roof was very high and circular and unlike the rest of the adjoining underground, it was a normal watchtower. Normal though much taller. As the upper parts of the castle can be seen from above so could the two watchtowers. Two spires emerging from the ground east and west of the Machiavellian-fort. The whole castles layout was strange and travelling through it oft magical. Long staircases could shrink, short ones extend, though always unheeded leaving a traveller early or late or none the wiser. Her last thoughts before mental readjustment were surrounding the unlikelihood she would see the under-castle again, so much to miss, so much unexplored. She'd even miss her hallways;

'Never see another wall-mood...the place will live on without me...I hope it lives... I hope we do...'

The place looked cramped and this due to an elephantine beauty, one that demanded any eyes first acknowledgement. Burning bright at the centre of the room, head down and hunched uncomfortably to fit the space, was a phoenix; made of ethereal fire it was the reds, oranges and yellows of flame, which shifted, though its impressive golden aura did not. Even silenced and stationary its dominance was breath-stealing. Although the room was filled with its fire, it was a ghostly one and did not strain the eyes like its rumoured father the sun did. The mystical phantasm was so large its wings pressed firmly against and covered much of the two walls, scarring and smouldering their stone. They easily blocked both windows, ash spurting occasionally through each. The fire-form so eldritch and supernatural it could not be absorbed by such empty rancid creatures. Their magic was given and easily stripped by such a thing. Stood directly under the phoenix in-between its ankles holding fist directly above head with straightened arm was Candez.

The bird was semi-corporeal as well as was being generated by the rumbling fractal coal-egg Candez held in right hand. If squinting, good eyes would see the tiny vortex wisps that emanated from the egg fed its physic incarnation. This was merely the projection of the foetal beast, which had clearly lived before and had awareness before its birth. Sophia could see its curious blue and red clashing colour through finger as he held it. She had only seen it properly with extended eye once and that's when the proud little Sun-twat was subtly forced by Yenya to display it, or him, as Candez scorned everyone at the time about. Spinning within so many moments of madness the girl couldn't recall the birds name.

The teenage boy was protective over his familiar, as well as everything else he owned. He stood straight-backed, accentuating his height, he was even taller than Yenja, only smaller than Zarros. His pallid chestnut hair stuck to his forehead from sweat and his thick brow was furrowing deeply into his pale face, his nose Anglo and sharp but so small his face would be boring if not for his eyes. His face was a canvas for them, a stage. It was not their size; they were small too, but they were a strange mixture of blue and green, mazes to ensnare. Combining; the comparison made his pupils seem darker and he weld them with deadly scope. His bottom lip was ample but top lip thin; making it akin to an archers bow. Perfect for a mouth that could fire deadly intention from any distance.

He had a long neck but kept his head low and compressed to compensate as well as choosing clothes well. Currently, a blue collared shirt of twinned material one denim one unknown with the buttons fancy doubloons and the top button a swirling emblem of bronze. The collar thicker on one side, giving a regal vibe, well dressed. Its tan brown of body but lighter red brown of pocket and thick collar. His clothes colours were synchronous furthering his ambiance.' He must have been fighting the blood-witch realised. He looked injured. Since battle now he had a thin clean lined scar across his right cheek, as well as many thin ones on the neck and most notably, though he wore it well, a deep scar going downward across both lips, off centre of the middle of his top tip it made his bow look loaded with arrow.

Before now the girl had only seen him clean-shaven but now, she sore his stubble was reddened. Whether it be because he was the heart of such a potently poignant scene or Sophia seeing him breaking his breath for the first time when usually so calmly arrogant, or that he was currently the shield she needed…but the witch found him attractive. So, kingly-looking, most found him entrancing but she did not, not usually.

Her head returned;

'NO. Think of ol' house-mother Prima's words when warning her off chasing boys';

"Oh yeah he's good-lookin' gurl but so's the Devil, it's horns you gotta check for."

…and she was still right. A lot of her advice has done me well! First good I saw'.' Irrespective, he was holding back the tide and whilst she wouldn't have him know it the girl was happy to see him just as much as his capabilities.

Biologically abundant innervation gave the blood-witch a rapid inner-voice and therefore oft allowed her more "time" to think than many others possessed. Be that as it may time didn't stop for her, and seconds and minutes mattered most on a war-clock. Sight scrutinising past the sun-sorcerer to whom was left and what they were doing, she saw it really was subtly frantic. The twins weren't here. She double scanned to make sure though she knew her eyes were right the first time, her stomach always tightened when they were around. She had not seen them on the field with Zarros or the vanguard. 'They've probably got a task; it couldn't have been just collecting me needed... I take it Arthur's in charge? Where was Yenya's body?' She was sparked to push past her pointless postulations by Pannah pushing past her body. The moon-witch did move impolitely more haphazardly, blood dried to her face and hair, whole body limping she used her last to get close enough then jumped and slumped by Candez feet. He stared down until their eyes met and they held each other's gaze, but no words were spoken and after a moment she crawled behind him. Reaching back wall she slouched against it, an upright foetal ball before closing her eyes. 'She must be even more tired than me, well, my wounds aren't exactly shallow, it's the bandages but 'spose my vigour's far from collapse'. Arthur had popped head and assessed their arrival but not looked up since; he did not notice Pannah's debilitation as he was so busy at work on the floor.

"GrrrRRR-GGGRRRRAAAAHHHH" Annaluuk's tiny echoed-growl could not saturate the space but was enough to reach every ear in the tower.

It forced Sophia back into the room, she flicked head toward the little girl. The child was still the electric door though now her outline blurred with even more distortion. 'Annaluke ain't able to hold that form much longer... now it is hurting, if she finds out about Taj, she may even turn that pained fury on us... Maybe better she empties herself...Plus how long can Zarros and Cassandra hold it all back, didn't exactly look like they were winning and soon that... that meat-colossus's gonna be "ready".' Her mind continued its yo-yo'ing, now back to the room, she could no longer stew; it was time to know what Arthur was doing and why.

The old man was knelt upon knee stretching forward, leaning over and working on several complex sigils and spells. He wore strange attire she had not seen him in before, until now she thought he only owned basic sews and a rusty set of armour he could not wear. Whilst far from his former flame, he still exhumed enough conviction to control the terrified, he had organised the foot soldiers before. Over-top his worn grey tunic and brown patched-up leather trousers were sizeable strange shiny-black pods. The same colour as Zarros scorpion-mounts hide they too had green glisten. A shed exoskeleton had been fashioned into a tailored leathered armour. 'That must have been a funny interaction' the girl posited. The buggy-overlay had many scratched sigils upon it, mainly on the chest and shoulder pieces which were largest, they varied in size. Some of which were still glowing in their individuate ways. 'Between the two, he must be gettin' quite a few boosts.' The girl had the smallest sip of calming at she sunk further into his presence. Attached to the right shoulder-pod was a hanging bag which the retired warrior desperately went in and out of with his only hand.

He was entirely drenched and dripping in blood from the chest down as if splashed by a wave of blood but then dunked his head in water which with subsequent sweat cleaned the upper half off. He had many dents and gouges but most noticeable was a perfectly spiral wound covering a third of his face. Starting from the right-side bottom of his wide neck it rose to the right cheek and ear, it wept but did not flow; 'JEEZ! Lucky he's prepared... Doesn't surprise me'ctually, he was probably the first to know the attack and gear up.' Old people sleep less than the young the blood-witch went on to decide and she found her ancient master seemed to never sleep at all.

Peeling her minds-eye away from his injury the situation had her not reading it but seeing his face as humanly as ever; his sunken sun-striped honey-oak eyes were puffy, his big nose another crook added, high cheekbones gaunt and once anvil jaw covered by the thinnest skin. His deep wrinkles many and the pale of age sprinkled by the pinky-red of broken vessels covered him all; 'Paler than usual' the girl dejected. 'Probably just shed too much blood... but maybe something more'. Nor girl nor witch had ever seen such an expression on his face, or more-so interpreted and identified the emotions it represented. Arthur did not feel fear or at least did not show it. More of a worrier but this looked to the blood-witch like as close as his face could get to such. He flicked countenance to Sophia and attempted smile, it failed, the half-moment fleeted as he thrust a knife back into his shoulder-bag. Hand returning with a Crowley-stone he returned attention to the floor and seemed to work even quicker. She finally allowed herself to properly engage, she closed the gap between her and the group, dropped head and gazed his works.

The man was guardedly creating two sigils; the one on the left she did not specifically recognise but known she had seen it before. Form gave a way to interpret it just like knowledge of Latin could unlock unknown English word. The one nearest to him was a protection spell of sorts, closer to himself than the other, it was smaller, completed and clean of blood. Any of which had come close had been hastily redirected by makers-smudge as to not activate the thing; It was reasonably sized, around 40cm by 40cm. Hefty sigils utilised charmed items as well as human-fuel and at very centre of this one was a long thin white feather. The plume-relic was within a circle which was within triangle, both within large octagon; though its outlines extended off itself to give it flowery visage. Attractively complex enochian shapes were within all 3 sections, all with visually pleasing ambigram-symmetry and style. Sigil calligraphy of this level arduous and awkward but not for Arthur. However, the second... It was the most complex sigil Sophia had ever seen, bar the forbidden one in Arthur's diary; it was God-level;

It took up a large area, in fact most the floor behind Candez 'n' Phoenix, just to the left and it was astonishing; 'It looks 99 layers deep for fuck-sake.' The blood-witch realised she didn't know as much as she thought, she couldn't even work out what this spell did. Her further thinking; 'Not even enough blood in the room for that, surely'. It was geometric in nature with so many shapes merging to form others so mazed the eyes. Lines did not stay within their stratum, so it did not have the angelic simple beauty of the first sigil but instead forced as if rose cross bred dei ameth. So much forbidden art. There was as much dark symbology woven within as light and her eyes widened at the idea of what size catastrophe a mistake would cause. So dangerous. It could have been a lesson and an exam; nonagons, decagons, conical fusions of Solomon-squares housed in hexahedrons and more formed the outer third. Deeper, it was hexagramix sigillium; 3 sets of 9 squares making 3 many point stairs whose lines extended to form crossovers. Worryingly, at centre was a blade-less handle. The hilt looked to be made of frozen blood, a reddened glass with much imperfection. Many semicircle curves and corners on the guard and tang which were sharp enough to make it a weapon itself. Even if it had blade it would be unpleasant to wield; it did not look friendly but before the girl could summarise her thoughts into questioning words Candez shouted;

"SHE'S HERE! Okay-old-man DO IT!" His words were well pronounced but voice strained.

"NO! For a start Metzu and Memtay are not back yet." Arthur's retort a snap though displeased he still did not look up.

"FUCK the Twins!" He sucked in air and pushed the words through gritted teeth.

Whilst the men argued Sophia found a need to find comfort elsewhere, as usual. She subtly slipped hand into satchel to twiddle one of Querf's horns or forcefully scratch his knotty coriaceous skin. Starting to panic as he wasn't furled within, she pushed past books and artifact, hand starting too haphazard. All previous assumptions and inquiry were gone, all replaced with boiling desire. Unable to cool her head and avoid spill over she found herself a little girl again. Her anxiety flowed out before she could stop it;

"I've-forgotten-something" Sophie squeaked, unaccustomed to such tones coming from the blood-witch it caught all's attention, all except

Annaluuk.

"ARE YOU FUCKING JOKING SOPHIA!!" This time Arthur's head left his work, he looked right in her eyes. It shocked all as whilst always chastising he rarely swore and never shouted.

The outcry kept her quiet but spurned her back to herself. She started turning emotion to thought; 'Where is he? and Why!?' but before either of these beginnings birthed answers everything was interrupted by new arrival. A deep 'skreeeigh' punctured from outside in; something large. Candez recognising noise flicked egg-hand right and the giant flame-bird of old rose its right wing slightly, allowing the bottom of the window to have no fiery withstander. In flew squeak, having to bend wing to enter so big and fat he had grown on magic. The size of a normal pony, he landed on the floor sloppily, seemingly tired under its own weight. Both seen and unseen. As well as the bat another familiar entered. A little lark soared straight through the same gap before the phoenix lowered wing resealing the window. The tiny grey and black bad boy could be easily identified by the group as Yenya's familiar as the crest was gold instead of yellow. As well as the crown feathers being multicoloured and much longer than a regular lark. It did not ground but circled before landing on Arthur.

His bird's face was strange, it was so big of eye and small of beak, but nothing mattered to the eye other than its beautifully over-feathered wings and regal sized golden head feathers. It often had specks of blue luminosity; orbs falling and fading from it, only the best eyes could see them. Or those attuned to looking at magic.

137

" SQUEAK!" Pannah had mustered relieved squark of her own, she was still weak but now pleased and eyes open. The bat crawled devotedly towards her.

" For Fuck Sake! Arthur Come-On." Candez was now pleading, frustration and shame alongside his petulance. He closed his eyes tightly after speaking.

Nobody but Sophia continued to watch the lark, it demanded deathly-attention with all but Arthur annunciating a shock after the bird had left the old-man's head flown to the centre of the room between Annaluuk and the others. Then flapping fiercely to float it opened its beak and words came out;

"Forgotten our lessons already my disciple?" It was Yenya's voice booming out from within the bird, much louder than the lark could naturally muster. Perfectly the same sound as if the icon was in the room.

Candez had opened eyes and mouth aghast but before he could have replied the Lark spoke again;

"Please have your familiar charge the sigil Pan" The bird did not look at anyone specifically as it spoke and Yenya's voice was cool, calm and composed.

Squeak was laying with head in the moon-witches lap, it did not enjoy being this full. Pam smiled and nodded into its face then at once, with one large wing beat flew over to the sigil. Landing opposite Arthur it began head-bobbing as if about to regurgitate then started spewing out blue sparkling-smoke. The more misted energy left him the smaller he got. As the mist entered the various shapes of the sigil, they glowed gold then didn't glow again, the next shapes turn. It patterned and pulsated, drinking in the magic. Once done the sigil had very faint permanent luminance. The bat now tiny, coin-size, slowly crawled back over to Pannah whom gently with sad-smile put squeak in her special breast-mounted container, before silently observing the room. Sophia couldn't stop her worst self-polluting mind; 'What the hell... is that truly him then or part of him? ... this is intense...but I don't care! I'm still getting MY familiar.' Her flagitious thoughts only Interpreted by Annaluuk.

The juvenile screamed a blood-curdle, now she was almost pure electricity in form of little girl. Her scream went alongside an electrical wave flux, so strong it melted then cracked the floor and walls as well as collapse the stairway. She then collapsed herself back to the little girl she was before. Steam emanated from her; her clothes burnt. After Sophia saw the little-un was down for the count she couldn't stop the continuation of planning her escape. She prickled; 'Still need to know what's happening and what the plan is... plus now can't get down the stairs...these people risked their lives for me... ill risk mine for Querf it's the same it's not insulting it's understandable.' The blood-witch walked over and picked up the little nature-witch in both arms, walking her over and around the bird, with duck, she placed the little girl propped up on Pannah who gave scrupulous look. Turning back to all else she spoke clearly;

"What's the battle plan why we not fighting?" After booming she placed hand on shoulder and rotated the other arm until it clicked then shook out her bones in faux preparation.

" Because we would lose." Arthur's response was quick and flat; not happy with his student's cockiness irrespective of the witch not being clear on the stakes yet.

"Fine. Well, I truly cannot hold on much longer Master." Candez only spoke so softly and polite to Yenya.

"We're going to need each other to 'win' as you would say. The twins are a crucial part of that." The Yenya-lark flew back over to Arthur's head after magical-vocalization.

"Okay okay okay." Candez spoke relenting, humming, he tightly shut eyes and jaw.

A small then paramount rumble rose from the ground, once rock-shake stopped a multi-sourced horror rumbled through the scraps of the entrance. 'That thing finally has a mouth huh'; Sophia had no fear left in her. Alongside this blaring, smoke starting seeping through the rocked-up staircase. Strange in colour; reddened beige. The fumes seeped from the tiny cracks, rising, it re-joined itself, swirling and growing. Once cloud had formed amongst a background of panic, a delicate and thin tornado descended from clouds centre.

" Shit". Pannah spoke in disbelief; Sophia pulled bracelet-blade.

"Calm it Sophia its them." Arthur spoke loudly but tiredly. Having finished both sigils he struggled to feet, using his hand to help himself up. He was every bit of a rusty old man, and he knew it.

The smoke tornado used its spin to throw parts of itself; it spun into new shape, the shape of snake. The snake chased tail, circling on the floor then from it rose two human figures. All three smoke-forms moved forward. As walking, growing more and more defined, when perfect, Metzu & Memtay as well as conjoining snake stepped fully formed out of the visage. Their misty remnants went grey and acted as normal smoke, dissipating. Now real, all could see Metzu and snake seemed fine but Memtay had received mortal wounds, though through magic they were now largely superficial.

The slender twins were no longer identical, when before few differences separated them; They both shaved their perfectly oval heads so religiously nobody knew their hair type or colour. They had reddish-brown skin from paleness being burned from them, healing amongst the sun too many times. Both had pierced brow, nose and lip though one twin wore silver rings whilst the other twin gold. Their teeth were awful, not in colour but shape; gap ridden and sharp. Snakes with alligator teeth. Further distinguished by eyes, both being purple though Memtay's slightly darker in shade. However now there were new differences between them. Memtay had missing left ear, it appeared to have been bitten off, as in its place was circular teeth marks and gouges. An over-thick mass of scars was on his neck from a hole in throat quickly healed. His broken nose now hooked and fat whilst Memtay's still thin and pointy and interestingly of all; looking like it should have been amputated was his left hand which was now burned charcoal black. The twins' clothes remained the same, full black one-pieces of shiny stretchy material. Varying slightly Memtay over-top wore a backpack and had hip-mounted weapons whilst Metzu had a bum-bag around waist. Indistinguishably tall and slim Sophia deduced a strength charm at play. The twins moved. Their snake stretched to accommodate as Metzu strode over to Arthur and handed him something whilst Memtay remained still.

The battle-worn twin then threw a marble sized item over shoulder blindly, Metzu caught it with frown and slipped it into bum-bag. He then turned to face Sophia who had long noticed one arm was behind his back.

" Shame only one use left now." Metzu spoke with over embellishment even danger could not change this. His voice was smug but smile genuine, half-warm from a closed-mouth.

The charm-wielder then tossed Querf toward Sophia. The gnome did not roll or flail but moved through the air lifelessly, she braced her catch, he landed softly in her arms.

SQUEAL "QUERF!!!" Sophia's voice broke and she felt like she wanted to cry.

Her friend was badly hurt, covered in scratches and his strange white-grey blood. So shocked was she the girl had not started comforting or questioning but just stared at him sadly.

"Tried to get the body, I I failed, I'm sorry..." Head tucked to chest

Querf's whispers were pain-filled.

Before Sophia could say anything the in-need gremlin slipped Taj's bracelet on her bare wrist and gained an enormous pleasure pulse reward. This not only helped the pain but pushed him into delectation. Sophia lowered him into her satchel, Comatose but with smile. The blood-witch decided when able she will lock him there by spell or even lock and key. Keeping hand in bag stroking him for both of them she settled on 'maybe just a lock for the bag'. She then looked up noticing now both the twins were talking to Arthur and Yenya who were nodding. Sophia jumped as the first sigil was activated whilst she was phased out and the white barrier around them shining into existence caused her eyes to refocus. Drawn to Candez she subtly observed him as the phoenix rescinded.

" Okay all of you, gather 'round" Arthur sounded significantly more tired than mere moments ago.

" Listen up my young adults. We're leaving this realm. Prepare your stomachs." Yenya-lark spoke warmly but with authority or as much as could be given to something on someone else's head.

Sophia' glare went unnoticed by Candez whom taking the moment of thinking he was unseen placed his coal-egg away into pocket. He then started observing and nursing his hand which had the most curious burn on it. Regardless of its unusualness it wept excruciation. When he spotted her, he hid his hand up his long sleeves. His other hand receded too so to not appear odd. Before her thoughts could fire, they were, interrupted by Yenya-lark;

"So-Phia listen." His voice was slightly pleading, and the bird left Arthur's head and landed on her shoulder before continuing.

" Were coming back with reinforcements, to ease the load." The voice leaving the bird was back to one of self-assurance.

"From the Gardener?" Pannah made religious hands to accompany her chiming query.

All ignored her.

"We're going to freeze time and go'get ANYTHING that can help." Arthur did not sound disappointed in Pannah but discomfited.

" Only all of us dying or coming back through the torn gate will restart it. Everybody make a que by Arthur and he will mark you." After giving order the bird flew back to Arthur's head. It gave a little peck after landing.

Removing the third jewelled eye from the stone demons face he had been handed Arthur whispered to the timeless relic and laid it out it on the floor looking up. The other two eyes and mouth glowed, and the relic melted becoming liquid. An ugly frothy puddle on the floor, thick like oil but bubbling. Each bubble stunningly opalescent but releasing sulphur upon popping. It stunk. Nobody looked happy with it, but everyone passed the two masters and received the mark; by being burned on the forehead. All winced except Annaluuk, who was still unconscious and carried by Candez. The burns faded leaving the smallest tattoo of the demon face on each head which then faded too. Sophia, last in line, grabbed the worried-warrior's wrist as he raised stone to her.

" Let's give them a moment." Yenya-lark after tweeting rose high into the air as high as the barrier would allow before letting gravity drop him, flying straight through the middle of the portal-puddle, he was gone. Instantly Candez followed his Master with Annaluuk in arms. Pannah gave one more look to the two then held breath and jumped in also. Now they were alone.

" Ya not coming?" The witch sounded melancholic and looked confused.

The master handed his student his diary though now it had thin web-like chains wrapped around it.

"So much I wish you could know but you're not ready." The melancholy was in his voice too now.

"I am... Wait know what?" The girl lost all emotion from her voice replacing it with suspicion.

" The chains will break when they need to. Please start at the beginning, last promise n'all". The old man smiled but did not look in her eyes.

" Jus' come". She was beseeching now, only stopping attempt at eye contact when loud rumble moved the rubble in sight.

" You're not thinking straight. You know big spells cost big and I'm no

Sophia." His smile only turned toothier at her confused face as he finally looked into her eyes which caused his own to well up.

He went to cut his scarred stump already tens of fresh wounds on it, but Sophia grabbed his wrist again. She instead pricked her finger with bone-needle and with single drop of blood the sigil activated. Arthur gave her slight shunt backwards before dropping to knees in front of it. It burned so bright it couldn't be viewed long but then inverted to a peculiar black glow. Unlike anything Sophia had seen. The ceremonial knife-less handle spun manically amongst art then stopped facing Arthur and raised to chest height. Levitating there a blade made of what she could only call time appeared. Off the black hilt, it slowly began moving towards Arthur, slowly piercing the chest; It desired his heart. The more it travelled into him the more everything slowed down.

" Thank-you master, you're the closest to a father I've had". Voice shuddering the girls' eyes were sincere and he could see she had love for him.

Finally, Arthur broke, he choked up and cried, he swallowed his tears sharply, the pain helping and hindering. He spat his final advice;

"Don't follow Yenya blindly, they're there to help YOU, not that they all know that". Arthur was measured but Sophia could hear the displeasure. As he looked away, she guessed he was recalling memories.

" Surely, it's not that 2D!?" The blood-witch grabbed her head to stop it spinning, her words breathy.

" No, no its not, it's not". He gave his student an encouraging wink. Tone alluring to being impressed at her returning wisdom.

The witching-blade halfway in, it had broken rib with wrenching crack and was about to enter his heart. The knight could no longer be present, the old man surfaced; he winced in such dismay that Sophia welled up. She had never heard him suffer like this.

"Go girl, go now.... And know I'll miss you". Arthur's struggle saturated him. The demand was barked but the love came surd.

She cried loudly, she stepped backwards towards the puddle, her body refused to turn its back on him. Finally, her foot did not find floor and she hopped backwards. It didn't feel like a portal, it was so much more unpleasant. It felt though she was un-sewn, and the thread pushed through a slit then re-sewn at the other end. The mind slingshot into this woven body; not her stomach but her mind threw up.

'Where is everyone!?' "Heeellllo!!!?" Her distressed voice echoed out into nothingness, or so it seemed. Sophia found herself in pitch darkness, a dark without moonlight. Suddenly, her foot stung then again and again. The floor was biting her! 'THIS AINT RIGHT!' her crying became full anxious weeping. She heard the noise of something fast approaching. 'I need to see'. With thoughts of Taj in the tree she worked blindly, she cut herself deeper than need across upper arm, smearing her hand with blood she painted directly onto her stomach. She began to levitate; she felt the floor try to keep her there by its mouth, but shoe came off and she was released. She levitated there, in darkness, crying, not knowing what to do.

END OF VOLUME 1.

up next: Sophia learns more of the truth, Yenya's morals are tested and secrets come to life as the gang tries to cross the first realm... The gap.

Epilogue: Imp-Ending Doom

'I'm always doing things I don't want to do, for things others need. All with my veneer shifting… its always to get what I want… I need…if they knew the truth.' Querf's inner voice was flying wild. The gremlins larger hand went from itching a broken horn on his head with finger and stub-thumb to tightly grabbing it as he ran, the pressure popping the veins out, up to the wrist. His anxiety was all consuming, he had to squeeze muscle and limb to contain it all, his double life always running on a damoclean edge; 'how did everyone not know...' As the ignominious ginormous mitt was dragged down his face the imp winced a muffled whimper; before quickly slamming palm into the well-polished marble ground, stopping sharply.

Panting he considered the distance already travelled; 'I've run so far, a countries length. So tired, overworked, I'm beat but unbeatable.' His mind somehow quickened as his tiny body stopped. 'Chest feels webbed, itchy, *breath*. Skins feel'ng tighter 'nd tighter the longer this is taking'. The gremlin had to wait, though to it the experience was akin to one losing breath whilst clinging to last-air in a house of smoke. He could not be caught. It was as if everything, Every-Thing hinged on this. The sun rising was counting on him not to fall. Only a perpetual moment, barely a before and an ever-distancing after. As he waited, he become more aware of his physical form; the gremlins mind seeped into his body manifesting all its uncomfortability. He was becoming aware of this more and more as the seconds dripped. This stillness was agony for Querf; 'Querf'sgottsto move. 'l Will not wait Cannot wait. NO STOP *pause*… I'll would up in

Satan's stronghold without it'.

Querf stepped out from where he had been hiding, behind statue, now the noises have ceased. 'Finally, no BOOM's... don't want'a get caught up in that war, a small ice arguing with big fire, a mountain verses a snake. The girl would kill him!'. The gargoyle spun with obsession many times on the spot. Though scanning that the giants were gone these frantic motions were too much leaving Querf working-wonky as he began his arm-assisted monkey-run once again. His egg continued cooking too; 'will I always be like this. I'm doing it but barely for her. Bu' I could change any time I want, be anything I want... Or am I slave. Do I have choice or is character fate!?'.

The ancient imp had scuttled such haste it had already reached the end of its demonic run. Smile creeping up his face Querf pictured his reward. This idea watering his face the smile reached manic size as he forced a slow skid stopping himself. Right in front of the needed door, a test of threshold.

The joy-goblin then stopped himself in another way; 'NO!'. Angry at the loudest voice inside his thought-form assemblage he seized himself back. 'Focus!' He rammed the index finger of his rarely used little hand into his left ear hole and shook hand so violently his head shook with it then after delay, his body did too. Though from a pressure released like a dog's reflex from tickle; 'prepare, prepare PREPARE!'. His own internal infernals would have to wait.

Querf looked up at the door. This mission weighed heavy on the imp. He needed the right outcome to succeed, to get it. The longer without it the harder it was to focus; 'it's fine, it will happen'. The gremlin took breath, breath so deep it pushed his belly out, he pushed in on himself but did not expel so the pressure caused his eyes to protrude from his face. Holding funny form for a moment then breathing out he was finally reset and could think again. Behind this transition was the place. Where she said he'd probably fail.

The gremlin took a scrap from its colour-covered arm, a blue thick wool, then used arm-aided spring-jump, looped the scrap around the handle and fell back to foot holding it. Querf pulled the wool yanking the handle into use then misused his horned head to slowly push the door ajar.

Then utilising his oversized smasher, he reached through the crack. Releasing wool-scrap the gnome placed stretched palm flat forward on the floor and slowly like dancer raised feet and slowly cartwheeled into room through the gap. As his feet went overhead and found new floor the door shut behind him. He saw in the vast sea of decoys and infinite levels of corridors was peril. He was not alone. 'As if this aint 'ard enuff'. So much terror and tension froze the little twat even though the harmless danger had not seen him. Then before deciding what he saw he jumped high into the rafters but the power of such a leap had him heard.

Querf hung hidden amongst the ceiling rafters hitting himself in the face repeatedly with his little hand. The large was tightly grabbing the wooden beam above leaving the worried gnome hanging without footing. His earholes dilated to full size at sudden sounds shocking him back to his surreal surroundings; squawks and numerous bothered ruffles had the gremlin perform pull up with colossus-arm to look over-top, at what was hanging with him.

To the side from him or seemingly, were umpteen birdcages, all varying sizes. Some bear-sized some bitty & petite but all equally elegant. Gothic rose-gold with impossibly small statues of perfectly formed dead royals dripping down some of the metal strings that made their shape. All empty cages were clean to the extent of giving glimmer. The confused-Querf thought he heard the closest clean and empty cage whisper, inviting him in. Within the majority were birds of all kinds and apparently all ages. He spotted a very old vulture next to a cage with a young magpie; there was no discrimination. Some were too big for their cage's others too small. The gremlin could not stop his pondering of it; 'why dun'they jus' change cage…why would they stay in these prisons? Choooose it… Ya don't even all look happy.' His head spun around a full 360 like an owl before snapping around and fixing gaze on a chosen bird hanging close to him, he whispered at it;

"Fly off my friend!" His voice encouraging.

The bird blankly continued to look unhappy with his presence as if waiting for him to go and carry on its business.

"Okay fuckya ya fools! Poison yourselves, never see th' outside." Pissed in tone he forgot them.

He returned to the semi-present and the obstacle below; 'Querf'll jus' stay still, they'll forget, don't move, don't look….NO… think of the king of

eyes...im wrong... like he says to master '" Truth remains truth whether
its known or not"'. He decided he would have to fight it. Querf quickly
changed mind which filled with goofy-fear; 'fight the thousand face
protector of the cedar-knowledge... nonono... Plus I won't get IT!' The
gargoyles thought was ripped short by him hearing the room filling with
the booming roar of threat.

"WHO'S THAT!?" The interrogation creaky and broken.

"Shit" He uttered. Followed by an idea; 'Have to trick it'.

Querf swung back and forth gaining swing like a pendulum until reaching
the closest bird who had ignored his offer and when swinging enough to
reach it he swiped. He knocked it off its hook to fall below. He whispered
as he unhooked it uncomfortably with little hand;

"Fuck-ya then buddy." Venomous resentment on his tongue.

The birdcage fell whilst causing critter to screech with commotion and a
wave of activity begun below as the priceless cage shattered out of sight.
Querf used this distraction to leave his hidden vantage. Faster than human
Querf begun to move. Leaping arm-aided through the rafters then come
the smaller wood come the rooms edge like handlebars. He only caught
one glance below as he travelled the distance so quickly. He went through
a small square-hole in the top wall, creation unknown, possibly for the
birds to enter the second adjoining room. Arriving through said-hole
Querf finally saw what Sophia directed would be the final landmark and
at lengthy last where the item is.

He leapt from above, barrelling as bullet the cannon-imp hit the ground exactly where he wanted but so hard it made stone-thud and crumpled him. He peeled himself up instantly. Re-markedly non-phased and begun rummaging through the cobwebbed white-wood bookcase next to the statue of the glowing-bronze fat woman with three eyes. 'Blood of the Witch, Blood of the Witch' Slow and considerate at first but not for long, after moments he sped up, removing and gandering five books per second from the bookcase. He didn't see the value in what he mishandled. Over-shoulder flew; a heavy thick-spine gold book of royal secrets, the irreplaceable notebook of the Shadow-Slayer and even a title-less vantablack book covered in ember-red chains that imprisoned the mind of an evil witch. Luckily it remained shut. This was a special bookcase kept separate from the main library. The pile behind him growing larger he noticed the noises from the first room had entirely stopped. He turned head 180 to look without stopping the ransacking.

"FaFaFuck sake Need more-time more-time!" His tone was stressed, tempo far faster than ears enjoy.

His head snapped back; he looked down at the book in his hand. It was it!! 'What fuckin' luck…my pleasure token, Blood of the Witch Volume 2.' He drooled onto the tome, trapped in thoughts of joy. He was not keeping calm and focused but instead fixating, his mind a diver with oxygen narcosis swimming deeper into sunken abyss. Fortunately, this was punctured and his mind resurfaced due to directed yell.

The scrap-headed chump had not heard foot or door and the enemy was looking straight at him;

"I WILL EAT YOU…little querm!" The scary voice trailed off as Querf had already leapt and was steaming back to the apparent bird-hole.

Leaving private and entering the general library. He saw the mess but refused to connect the dots; cut the mental string himself; 'The room pfft, it's destroyed in here, something flying in the air… Place be crumbling, it's gonna crumble around me… Gotta'Speed'up'. He leapt over broken seat and ducked under angry peck and with poorly executed spinning spring dove for the silvered door. He reached it but not without grazing something. He refused to look back. This time he placed book into nano-hand and held it as tight as possible with its measly grip. He jumped; hung from the handle, turned it but held on then repeatedly thrust crotch against door, bouncing against it until opening it slightly. Querf swung his leg around and into the made gap to keep door open then let go, sliding down half in half out before scuttling away.

He took quarter-breath and continued; 'getting there, calm 'n' quiet through the big room, I gotta.' The dumb-eyed gremlin crept onward, looking around.

'So many crabs, fighting over the special-water. No, fighting over that new shell, an ample morsel, empty, but why?' Querf looked closer into himself; 'no the crabs aren't fighting their dancing! Swapping shells with each other… They're so busy they're not even noticing the biggest, best shell! Ya'know looks like there not even crabs!' He shook his head so much and so hard it hurt. He rubbed his eyes then poked them in, half a finger deep, it was only uncomfortable but would look painful to a man. He wiggled over and jumped on a nearby pillar and quietly wriggled up it in the oddest way. With so many people about and arguing about prophecy and sacrifice Querf decided to go a different way than originally planned.

'Lots of secrets in the room of water, secret doors and passengers Querf's pretty sure only he and the master of eyes know...'. The inconsistent-runt glad the voices were loud enough to give him cover pushed aside the ornamental head he knew hid secret and slipped into the magic-walls themselves.

With a Clink Clonk Bomp and a Bump he had made his way through and out a pillar snap-door right by the stone archway and hallway of doors, well past the consternation. 'SHOT Car those spots-are-tight'. This door was easier, so galactic the outer gap was thick enough for his fingers. He used his scrap-trick then when the handle pulled, he crammed his four bitty blighter's and stub-thumb in said perimeter and prized open the door. Tornado-twirling through he was finally on the home stretch; 'doorway-hall-doorway hall.'

Running down the impossible hallway the gremlin found himself slipping again, he had to look at the witchy doors, everyone did. He slowed his pace ever-so. He saw a door he wished he could look behind; A yellowish glowing midnight-swamp, mostly water, the veil impeccable glass. However, mossy growths had begun puncturing through the right corner cracking the barrier. Querf saw a thousand of his face in these shards then through them something moving in the swamp.

Another door caught his gaze; it unlike the others had no handle. The whole door crystallised fire. Red and blue but solid as rock. It still moved with the flicks of flame but 100 times slower and the imp couldn't help but want to know the hell behind it.

He saw another; the third was a seemingly normal holly wood, however it wore a symbol that gave the gargoyle a hallowed and deathly vibe as the longer he looked at it the more it glowed a silvery green. A triangle with a circle within and a vertical line running throughout all. His mind was getting overstimulated; 'this is so long I be running on the spot'. The doors begun to blur together. He blinked half a hundred times. Thinking of trouble 'Blue-broken hands erupted out of the ground and tried grabbing the delirious-gremlin, to pull him down, to hold him. He danced and stomped and squealed in fear.'

He forced change and this was replaced with Querf-thought of reward; 'The hands turned wooden and grew tall, their fingers separating and branching. Eldritch fruit started growing and stopped Querf struggling, he plucked and ate ones of the smiling apples. Whilst chewing and dribbling golden juice the trees and hands disintegrated into a wet pink mist.'

He opened his eyes but closed them as he continued running, to avoid temptation. Avoiding the feeling wall was ahead he finally felt the weird portal feeling, 'Booooiing'. Eyes were kept closed anyway until he bumped into something. Opening his imp-peepers he saw it was a marble showcase stand without a prize and was now wobbling. 'Yessss!' He saw he was in the relative safety of the common. A happy ballerina Querf put the book on his head flat for added difficulty then elegantly and perfectly one foot spun all the way to the red door, dodging all furniture and every fragile artefact. Snatching the stringed vial of Sophia-spit tied to his arm he saw there was one use left, he used it to unlock the final door to heaven.

'Hate these steps, so big, so not for me,' The imp hopped with great effort up the giant steps until his rhythm was interrupted by an unusual sight. A smell-less gas, creeping down the stairs growing closer to him, but it did not move like it should. Stranger still, the Smoke held a sound as it flowed, a symphony that could not be called a song but enticing nonetheless, alternating between the beautiful and the grotesque.

'Woah, forget that ab-shite I've run so far, travelled the earth 'nd nearly done, why stop.' He ran through himself and up the rest of the stairs, as he moved, he ripped a flower from the wall; a perfect peony with a million petals each of them curling up in on themselves and out again with a staggered timing forming gorgeous patterns. He regarded it before stuffing it into his mouth and chewing it up. Finally, he bust back into Sophia's room who did not notice due to being halfway through a debate with Taj.

The imp saw the energies; 'power versus love. He's using his smile as shield, against a barrage like that it won't last long". He watched and listened rather than reveal himself, a regular ploy of his.

"Happiness may seem weaker than blue, purple or any type of pain. But sadness is fleeting from future and one day Soph even your sad memories will hold no sway over you, instead they might even get you smiling." Taj spoke with the utmost earnestness and grinned with cheek as he awaited retort.

However, no retort came as the blood-witch had noticed her familiars return and therefore the private bartering was over;

"Okay! Later Taaaj!". The last word was elongated, mouth pursed, brow furrowed; Her friend did not fight her invitation to leave.

Taj noticed Querf who scratched his armpit and burped. Deepening his smile, he said nothing but turned and left, buzz however did not; the shin sized and puppy plump Kodiak Bear that had been running around his legs continued its dogged path. Taj's movement did not stop its circling and he passed through him a ghost. The young'uns familiar's only known USP being phasing. After three more circles alone each smaller than the last it stumbled over itself and rolled forward before looking towards its leaving master. The metallic-olive bear was 25 per translucent, just nearly of full form. It bound off happily and carefree after its master, ignoring Sophia & Querf. Taj ignored him back but threw up his hand in a silent goodbye to the blood-witch. Sophia turned to her familiar, it took the opportunity to speak first;

"You two be sweet, I rec." Only half taunting the other half sincere he was interrupted none the less.

"Okay okay, give me it!" Her tone demanding, truly his maser she held arm out hand flat to receive.

He handed her over the book which she did not swipe but took softly, Sophia turned patted his head like a pet and walked off towards windowed balcony. Querf stayed still like a pet awaiting reward, his proportional pulse of pleasure; 'it's here, it's gonna be huge I 'ope.'

" Wrong Book Idiot! This is Blood of the Witch Volume 2; I need Volume 1!" A higher pitch than usual. She huffed in frustration, threw the book on her bed, quite the distance it had to fly.

"Such a simple task yet I knew you were too quick to have got it right. *pause* Did you bump into a Master? Or that miserable librarian?" Now looking at him from afar, the hands on the hips pose and tilted head said as much as a shout.

"NOOOO" He fell to his knees. "Also No." He was lying but too quick for her to catch, no time for her to spot it as she was still thinking on Taj. Even quick minds need to churn shit up. 'How!? I never get away with lying'. The gremlin quickly filled the silence hence she gazes things deeper.

"AYYYYYHHUU so-so-so I'm without it, instead so much depression" Over dramatic he spun around then fell, a theatre death.

"It's Biochemistry squirt, don't worry, you-de get resistant, tolerant, if you always got the hit. Now you been refreshed, you'll get to remap those braincells. The next buzz will be particularly good now." Comfort in her tone it was an honest shot at placation for her half-friend. The gremlin missed the nuance;

"You have Decorum but no restraint Soph!" Frustration still flowing from his voice he took wobbled run, speeding up as it went towards the door. Not knowing where he was going his heart was just palpitating with an addict's disappointment.

"Still reeeaaally need that book bud." She did not even turn to see, knowing it a treat the imp could not resist. The elongation almost cocky.

'So, it begins again....'

Printed in Great Britain
by Amazon